Icy Passage

By

Shawn McConnell

for Casey and Kyle

Acknowledgements

I would like to thank Claudia McConnell for delivering me to Hoonah, the only place I have ever wanted to call home.

A special thank you to my wife, Teresa, for the infinite edits. I would also like to thank my good friend and sometimes editor Bob H. for taking the time to read and offer his suggestions.

This is a work of fiction, though some of the places described refer to and resemble actual places, the characters, names and events are all fictional. Any resemblance to actual persons is purely coincidental.

Copyright © 2017
By
Shawn McConnell

Prologue

The children were snugly tucked into the tiny bed, a heavy patchwork quilt pulled tightly under their chins. Their bright eyes sparkled in the dim flicker of the oil lantern.

The old man sat perched on a stool that seemed a toy beneath his great frame. His beard was a magnificent gray bush. The woolen threads of his greatcoat were frayed at the sleeves and the knitted cap he wore low over bristling eyebrows was more worn than the coat. The pale, green eyes that peered from under the cap were full of life and yet wizened from many years spent at sea and in the Siberian forests.

Outside the frosted window another of Mother Winter's storms picked at the cracks between the heavy logs. The fire in the hearth below sent shadows dancing across the ceiling timbers. Eerie moans and an occasional whistling rose and fell over the crackling of the fire.

"Grandfather, please, oh please, tell us the story of *The Boy*," a tiny mouth beneath coal black eyes implored the giant on the stool. The small girl's voice was little more than a squeak.

"Yes, please tell us of *The Boy*," the request was echoed by a red cheeked boy with a thick mop of blond hair. His green eyes were sharp, like the old man's, and he listened intently to the sounds, which swirled around the cabin.

"Hah," the old man laughed loudly. "Surely you don't want to hear that tired old tale."

"You know we've been waiting years for that story, grandfather," the little girl reminded him. "Tell it to us now, we aren't going anywhere."

"Very well then, but should you fall asleep I am going down by the fire to read my book," the old man warned.

"You will fall asleep before we do." The boy challenged his grandfather.

The old man slipped off his coat and lay it across the foot of the bed then set his wool cap on the coat.

"That should keep your toes warm while you listen."

He sat back on his stool and rested his broad shoulders against the curve of the logs and began...

Farewell

Chapter 1

The women carried woven baskets that hung beneath them as they moved over the rocks near the water's edge. Each used a knife to pry small creatures from cracks between the rocks. A light fog hung in the air nearly hiding the women as it swirled in from the open sea.

In the distance a large wooden canoe was pulled up on the shore. Two men leaned against its high bow. Their brown faces, crisscrossed with black tattoos, were visible below thick black hair that reached to their shoulders. The men stood, watching the women gather food. They made no effort to help the women and did not speak to them as they filled their baskets. They men scanned the shoreline and the edge of the forest frequently. Two heavy spears were propped in the bow of the canoe.

The boy lay on his stomach. The thick moss that carpeted the forest floor was wet with dew. His canvas jacket and jersey were soaked through. Tucked between the trunks of two giant trees, he had a sweeping view of the beach below and the sound that stretched to the horizon. Dozens of tiny islands were scattered about. Dark, rocky shorelines ringed the stands of green trees that covered each of the islands.

The boy breathed down the front of his coat to conceal

the mist that his breath caused in the cool air. After watching the women for a moment he turned his attention to the canoe. The two men had vanished and the spears were gone. His heart bounced. He scanned the shoreline. He had been careful not to peer too far out from his cover, but perhaps he had been seen. If so, the Kolosh warriors would certainly come after him. The Kolosh hated Russians.

He slithered backward, rising to his knees when he was below the edge of the cliff. He stood and looked through the forest in the direction of the canoe. Seeing no sign of the men he broke into a trot, picking his way between the tall trees. He moved silently on the thick moss as he descended toward the beach. Halfway to the shore he stopped and held his breath, training his ears in the direction of the canoe.

A twig snapped. He froze and cocked his head. He saw movement at the edge of a thicket down the hill to his right. The Kolosh.

He ran down the hill and stumbled as his foot sank into a hole in the moss. He staggered to his feet and sprinted for the beach.

As he approached the shore the forest brightened. The broad and jagged leaves of the devil's club plants were splattered with golden light.

At the edge of the woods he crouched behind a fallen tree. He listened to the sounds of the shore and the forest. Birds chirped out morning songs and the insects were beginning to buzz. He felt beads of sweat trickle down the inside of his shirt.

Out of the corner of his eye he caught a flash of movement between two trees, closer than before. His heart was racing as he plunged into the thicket that separated the rocky shore from the tall timber.

The boy dashed to a pile of branches and tossed them

aside, uncovering his baidarka. The light shone through its skin covering, revealing the neatly shaped ribs of the sleek boat. He lifted the baidarka and ran down the beach. He glanced over his shoulder checking for the Kolosh warriors. The jagged rocks hurt his feet.

He dropped the baidarka into the shallow water and pulled his paddle from inside of the boat. He pushed away from the shore and slipped into the round opening in the center of the boat. He used the end of the paddle to push into deeper water and dipped a few shallow strokes to move away from the shore.

The Kolosh emerged from the thicket and stood watching as the boy paddled away from the shore.

When he was a safe distance from the warriors, he stopped paddling and turned the bow of his boat to face the open sea. Tomorrow he would begin a journey that would take him beyond the horizon.

The tall cone of a sleeping volcano towered above the huge island to the west. Beyond its southern slope lay the open ocean. To the west, far too distant to imagine, was his new home, Russia.

The sound was coming to life. The wind stirred ripples on its deep blue surface. Seabirds of all shapes and sizes hurried about in search of their favorite fish. High overhead a pair of eagles circled gracefully, scanning the water below for a meal. The boy closed his eyes and let the sounds and smells fill his senses. The memories would keep him company in the months ahead.

When he could delay no more, he swung the bow of the baidarka to face the sun and paddled toward the fort at New Archangel.

Chapter 2

The log walls that ringed the fort were hewn from small trees. A cluster of piers lined the waterfront. Behind the piers was a row of trade shops and warehouses. A muddy track wound along the shoreline connecting the buildings, forking near the main pier toward the fort's tall gate. Behind the walls of the fort, New Archangel was making ready for the day's work.

When the boy pulled his skin boat out of the water and lifted it over his shoulder, a deep sadness filled his heart. He carried the boat up a beach of small rounded stones. Under the main pier he lowered the baidarka and tipped it up against a log wall. That would keep it from filling with water until his father came to collect it. He studied his baidarka carefully. He knew every knot in the sinew that bound the joints and it hurt deeply to leave his prize behind. His father had explained from the beginning that there would be no use for the little boat at the Naval Academy, nor would there be a way to transport the boat overland from Petropavlovsk to Saint Petersburg.

This would be his final moment with his beloved boat.

He took the paddle in his hand. His father had allowed him to take his paddle with him on his voyage. He had carved the paddle from a single plank of spruce and it was painted with the things he loved the most about his home; a deer and bear faced each other on one side of the blade and a raven and eagle covered the other.

As he climbed the steep slope from the beach to the narrow track, he gave one last glance back at his baidarka.

The walk to his cabin was long and uphill. The rain from the night before had soaked into the ground leaving the mud dried with the deep ruts from the wheels of carts that traveled the path.

The tradesmen were making their way to the waterfront. They would fashion the rigging, fittings and tackle that were needed to keep the ships of the Russian American Company moving to and from the ports of the world. The loads of sea otter and fur seal pelts the ships carried to Russia brought a high price in the markets of Canton.

His father would already be at his shop, stoking the furnace and readying the iron for his work as blacksmith. His father had an important job in the fort. He made a good living and was provided a comfortable cabin near the forest at the edge of the fort.

"Son, I don't wish to see you beating steel into hinge pins when you are my age," his father told him. "You will go away to the naval academy and learn to be a sailor."

"But father, I don't want to be a sailor. I enjoy the small boat and being around the workmen. I think I would make a good blacksmith, maybe I will even be as good as you some day," the boy would reply.

"Nonsense," was his father's stern response. "Your education is more important. Father Nikolai says that you already know more than he does. He cannot teach you anymore. Your mother made me promise that you would go away to school. I will keep that promise."

"Why can't I wait another year?" The boy asked each day.

"Another year will put you further behind in your studies. Now, no more of this talk. The arrangements have been made and you will go."

The conversation always ended the same way.

The boy made his way up the winding path that led through the heart of New Archangel. The gates had been opened for trade and soon a Kolosh trading party from the village north of the fort would bring in their furs. The Kolosh were only allowed in the fort early in the day, and then only in small groups.

Governor Baranov had a healthy respect for the ability of the Kolosh to make war. Baranov's first mission to establish a fort on the sound ended when the Kolosh attacked and drove the hunters back to their boats and back to Kodiak.

Smoke rose from the chimneys of the cabins that lined the path, drifting lazily on the gentle breeze. The cabins were simple, rugged and uninviting.

The boy reached the end of the trail and turned to look down over the fort and the dome and cross on the church. On a tall hill at the water's edge stood the fortress-home of the Governor, Alexander Baranov. The stout building commanded a view of the entire fort and the docks. It was the largest building in the fort.

Baranov was a legend. Tough and determined, he had built New Archangel into a prosperous port city and the much-loved capital of the Alaska territory. Ships from all over the world called in the harbor. Some came from as far away as the Sandwich Islands, bringing with them stories of sand beaches and lush jungle islands. The boy loved to roam the docks, listening to the sailors' tales.

He looked over the town spread below him and saw things he hadn't noticed before. Today, everything seemed special.

The boy turned and walked the final twenty paces to the cabin at the end of the trail. The gray logs with moss stuffed between them seemed shabbier than before. The moss and grass on the sod roof were tall, a whole summer of growth behind them.

He gathered an armload of firewood from a stack beside the door. The pile of firewood had been greatly reduced. The boy thought of his father gathering firewood alone, doing the job that the boy had shared with him since he could carry a block of wood.

A single tiny window at the front of the cabin let in a small amount of light which shone on the iron stove against the back wall. The cabin was still warm but the fire his father had stoked for breakfast tea had faded. He opened the stove's heavy door and stirred the glowing embers. He tossed three pieces of wood into the stove and shut the door, sliding open the vent to give the coals some air.

He turned back to the table to light a lamp and could hear the crackle of the wood as the fire came to life. He sat quietly as he waited for the kettle to warm. His father's long gun hung above the door on two wooden pegs. It was a simple weapon but his father had instructed him in its use and he was a proficient marksman. He was disappointed that he would leave New Archangel without having taken his first deer with the gun.

When the kettle began to whistle, he made strong tea and dipped pieces of black bread in the steaming brew. The bread dissolved in his mouth, and trickles of the bitter tea ran down his chin. He wiped his mouth on the sleeve of his coat. The sleeve was still wet and smelled of the forest. He was glad. He would smell the coat on his trip to Russia to bring himself back to the forest.

He moved about the cabin, packing his belongings into a canvas bag. A knife, extra clothes, a comb, his tin of char cloth and his flint and steel all went into the sack.

When he had his travel pack ready he left it on the table and walked down the hill to the church to say good bye to Father Nikolai and the other students. Everyone at the school wished him a safe voyage and told him that they would miss him. Seeing his friends and schoolmates made him yearn to stay in New Archangel even more.

He left the church and slowly made his way up the hill to the cabin just before the sun went down for the day. He was asleep in bed before his father returned from his shop.

Chapter 3

The boy was awakened by the rattle of the kettle. The cabin was cold and dark. The chill of the late summer air seeped in through the gaps between the logs. He pulled the heavy quilts up over his head. His mother had sewn them when he was a tiny boy and they had served him well.

He could barely remember his mother's face, pale but beautiful. Long black hair pulled back in a single braid. She had fussed over him in his bed, tucking the blankets tightly around him and singing him songs. She died of a fever in the winter of his seventh year. His father had been very good to him, but both of them missed her terribly.

He could hear his father stirring the coals and feeding the fire. He waited for the heat to reach the loft before he slid out of bed and dressed. He folded the heaviest of the quilts into a neat bundle and tied it with a short piece of rope that hung from a peg above his mattress. The quilt would be his sole source of comfort during the cold nights to come.

He climbed down the ladder. An oil lamp on the wooden table illuminated his father's face. His father had a thick, black beard, bushy eyebrows over dark brown eyes and wavy black hair trimmed above his ears. He pushed a cup of tea across the table. The boy nodded his thanks and took a seat. They ate bread and jam and sipped their tea, each taking his turn looking about the dimly lit cabin and staring into their steaming cups.

"We should go," his father announced.

"Yes papa," the boy replied. He rose and rinsed his cup in a basin of water and turned it upside down on the wooden table. He collected his travel pack and bedroll and stood by the door. He took one last look around the only home he had ever known and then stepped into the darkness.

New Archangel was still fast asleep. His father joined him on the porch, and put his hand on the boy's shoulder. They made their way down the dark path by the faint twilight that hinted of the day to come.

At the end of the trail a burly man with a stoop to his walk pushed open a wooden door cut in the heavy walls of the fort and let them pass. The harbor was already alive with activity. The decks of the *Irena*, a double-masted merchant ship, were lit with oil lamps and her crew was busy making preparations to set sail.

As they approached the ship the boy stood back as his father made his way to the loading ramp and spoke with a man carrying a list in his hand. The man nodded and looked at the boy. His father jerked his head in the direction of the ship and the boy slowly moved forward. His feet were like stones and resisted his urging. He wanted to run, to take his small boat and flee to the islands. He moved forward and stood beside his father. The man on the ramp crossed onto the deck and disappeared.

His father put his hands on the boy's shoulders and looked him up and down.

"Take care of yourself, son," he said in a soft voice. "Your grandfather will be waiting for you when you get to Petropavlovsk." He handed Alexi an envelope. "This has your papers and a letter for your grandfather."

"Yes sir," Alexi replied. He stared at his boots.

"The cook is an old friend of mine and will look after you

on the ship," his father said. "He expects you to help him out to earn your keep but he is a good man. He will help you find your grandfather when you reach Russia."

He lifted Alexi's chin to look him in the eyes. "Son, you are the most important thing to me in the world. I know you are angry with me now, but I know you will be happy in Russia and I expect to see you here in four years' time," he hugged Alexi tightly to his chest and whispered one last thing into his ear. "A surprise will be waiting for you when you reach Petropavlovsk."

Tears rolled down Alexi's cheek and soaked into his father's coat.

"I love you Papa," was all he could manage.

His father held Alexi at arm's length for a moment, wiped his son's tears with massive thumbs and then turned him in the direction of the ship. He gave Alexi a gentle shove forward and turned and walked away. Alexi crept up the ramp and onto the bustling deck of the boat. He wiped the last of his tears from his cheeks and looked around.

A round man wearing a white apron emerged from a small cabin on the stern deck. He moved toward Alexi and said, "Come. Come with me and I will put you to work."

It was the cook. Alexi followed him back toward the small cabin. The sky glowed pink over the fort.

Irena

Chapter 4

When the sun appeared over the mountain behind the fort, the *Irena* was making way toward the cape below the volcano. The ocean swells lifted the ship in a steady rhythm. An offshore breeze filled the sails and heeled the boat to port. Alexi stood at the bow, watching the ocean grow larger. The islands had slipped behind and they would soon round the cape to begin their westward passage to Kodiak, the Russian American Company's main port. After stopping for supplies and fur in Kodiak, they would make the long passage west to Russia. It would be a dangerous voyage and even a sturdy vessel like *Irena* would be tested.

Summer was drawing to a close, and the storms of fall weren't far away. Alexi watched as the bow of the *Irena* sliced the waves, throwing sheets of spray to the sides of the ship. Her stem rose, water dripping from the planking, then plunged deep into the next wave, burying the bow half under water. The chill of the wind and the spray excited him. He felt the ocean, savored the smells, the sights and the sounds, and for the moment forgot about home.

When the rushing water had worked enough of its magic on him, Alexi went below to his quarters in the forecastle. The foc'sle was cramped and he shared the space with ten crewmen. His bunk was high against the ceiling in the point of the bow. He spread his quilt over the smooth planks and tucked his travel pack into the corner. A few crewmen slept in their bunks, snoring peacefully as the boat moved with the swells. He made his way to the ladder and returned to the deck.

The small cabin at the stern of the ship housed the galley, which sat atop the captain's stateroom and a cabin for company officers below deck.

The cook had set the rules for him when he boarded the *Irena*. The stern deck was off limits at all times. He was to be on deck only if he was crossing to the forecastle ladder or standing in the small triangle of space at the bow. The crew of the *Irena* would be scrambling in the rigging, trimming the sails to maintain maximum speed. The deck was for men, and he was not to be on it.

He crossed the deck quickly, pausing only to look through a wooden grating that covered the small opening in the main hatch. The faint light that stabbed into the depths of the hold revealed piles of gear, some tools in open barrels, and barrels of food and water to provision the ship's crew.

In the galley, the cook sat behind the dining table, peeling potatoes.

"Come, young man. I need help with these potatoes. The first few days at sea we eat well. Then will come the black bread and tea, when everyone is hardened to the work of sailing," the round cook motioned for him to take a knife from the table.

Alexi picked up the knife and a potato and followed the cook's example. In no time he was keeping pace with the bald man. Beads of sweat appeared on the cook's pink scalp. Neither of them spoke as they worked their knives and it soon became a competition. Peels were flying and the pile of potatoes grew. When the cook judged the mound of potatoes high enough, he took up a peeled potato and sliced it with three quick strokes. Six white crescents lay neatly on the table. He nodded to Alexi to follow his lead and the competition began again.

"Enough, enough!" the cook finally burst out, raising his knife to Alexi. "We have potatoes for fifty men. Now carry them to the heavy pot, there."

He pointed toward a large black kettle on the cast iron cook stove. Alexi transferred the potatoes to a large wooden bowl and carried them to the pot of boiling water.

"Gather up the peels and toss them over the side," the cook said without looking over his shoulder. Alexi scraped the peelings from the table and floor and piled them into the empty bowl. When he had every peel, he pushed open the galley door and crossed to the rail.

The wind was strong from the southwest and the *Irena* heeled to starboard. When he shook the bowl of peels high over the rail the wind scattered them far from the ship. The shower of potato skins was quickly swallowed by the foaming wake.

Alexi returned the bowl and took a seat at the table, watching as the cook prepared the soup. He added large pieces of salted meat and chunks of carrots. Soon the soup was boiling and the rich smell of the meaty mixture filled the galley. Alexi dozed.

A blast of cold wind woke him. Three crewmen tumbled into the small cabin and plopped down at the table. They spoke amongst themselves, taking no note of Alexi. He slid to the corner and listened to them describe the work of sailing. The southwest wind pushed the ship steadily toward shore, and the crew had to keep a constant crosswind course to keep from being blown ashore. The men were tired but excited, and Alexi began to look forward to one day working beside such men.

The cook ladled up a large bowl of soup for each of the men. He placed a loaf of black bread in the middle of the table and stuck a knife through it. The largest man, one they called Ivan, plucked the knife from the loaf and hacked several slices from the end. He speared each of them and set a piece of bread beside each bowl. The other two men nodded as they blew on spoons of soup, hurrying it to their lips. The cook returned with a pot of tea and heavy mugs. The men slurped their soup, ate bread dipped in the broth and washed it all down with mouthfuls of tea.

The men finished their meal and returned to the decks. A new group soon replaced them, and so it went through the middle of the day and into the evening. Alexi never moved. The men paid him little mind. The cook fed him and gave him tea and then instructed him on how to handle the dishes. Life aboard the ship was so organized it seemed magical.

The *Irena* slipped easily through the water and the shoreline soon vanished. In the distance, tall mountains, draped in a blanket of white, towered over green foothills. Alexi knew he had traveled farther this first day than he had in his entire life.

By the time darkness came, Alexi was exhausted. The fresh air, his work in the galley and the motion of the ship had sapped his energy. When the cook dismissed him, he headed straight to his bunk and was asleep soon after he pulled the quilt over his head.

The boy stood on the pier beside his father. They watched as the Irena was towed to sea by the longboats. Each of the boats was manned by men who set upon the oars like bears. The ship slipped silently into the distance, her sails slowly unfurling.

"Thank you for letting me remain in New Archangel, Papa," the boy said.

Chapter 5

Alexi's stomach woke him. He lay still, listening to the sounds of the men who were sleeping in the foc'sle with him. They had spent the night keeping the ship on course for Kodiak.

He slipped out of his bunk, balancing on the rail of the bunk below. As quietly as he could, he pulled on his trousers and tucked in his shirt as he made his way to the ladder. He staggered a bit as the ship broached on an odd wave, regained his balance and climbed the ladder.

The sun hit him square in the face as he pushed open the door and he had to squeeze his eyes to a slit. A steady breeze pushed gentle swells topped with tufts of white water. Rafts of seabirds and gulls moved around the boat, some of them following in the wake, shrieking as they dodged back and forth.

He breathed deeply and was reminded of the sound and his baidarka. The sea was a magical place indeed, he thought to himself as he stole across the deck to the galley.

The cook stirred a large pot of oatmeal, thick and gooey. The galley smelled of cinnamon.

"Good morning to you lad," the cook greeted him with a heaping bowl of oatmeal.

"Good morning sir. It is a fine day," Alexi replied.

"Thank you," he said, taking the steaming bowl from the cook's hands. He slumped onto the empty bench.

"How long to Kodiak?" Alexi, asked, his mouth full.

"It is not my business to keep our position, now is it?" The cook slid the pot of oats to the side to keep it warm. "No sir, I just keep everyone fed, and the captain he doesn't bother me."

"How many times have you made this voyage?" Alexi inquired of his new friend.

"More than I care to tell. But it is funny you should ask, since this will be my last," the cook leaned close to him and whispered, "not a word of this to the captain, mind you. If he finds out I intend to leave ship at Petropavlovsk, he'll lock me in my cabin until we heave anchor. Loves my cooking, he does."

The round man stepped away and slapped his hand on his thick stomach and laughed aloud. Alexi smiled back. He liked the cook. The cook had shared a secret with him.

"What will you do when you leave the ship?" Alexi asked.

"You certainly are curious aren't you?" he replied. "Well, since you can't escape I'll spin the whole tale for you," he sat down across the table and pulled his stained white apron from around his waist and laid it over the back of the bench.

"I have a farm near Magadan, a beautiful city on the Sea of Okhotsk. My wife and two sons keep the gardens and animals while I am at sea," he described the farm and its view of the sea.

"How old are your boys?" Alexi asked.

"They aren't mere boys. No, they are young men, both working on finding wives of their own, I hope," he laughed.

"They keep their mother company and look after her. None are finer than they; I can assure you of that," the cook swelled with pride.

The cook reached into the pocket of his shirt and pulled out a silver pocket watch. It was plain on the front, but when he opened the case, the inside glowed bright yellow.

"Is that real gold?" Alexi asked excitedly.

"As gold as the morning sun," the cook replied. He handed the watch to Alexi. The weight of the timepiece was impressive.

An inscription was etched in the underside of the lid.

"With all my love, Anna," Alexi read the words aloud.

"Anna. My Anna," The cook held out his hand for the watch.

"Enough talk. If you want another story you will have to earn it," the cook said.

He rose and opened the cupboard below the stove. He pulled out a large canvas bag and shoved it toward Alexi. "Take this into the main hold and fill it with potatoes and turnips. I will boil them for our soup tonight."

"How do I get into the hold?" Alexi asked. He didn't want to venture onto the deck without clear instructions.

"All you do is pull aside the small grating covering the hatch and climb down the ladder to the bottom. The barrels of stores are against the aft bulkhead. You can't miss them."

The cook made it sound easy, so he grabbed the bag and headed out the door. On deck he passed two men.

"Look, it's the cook's boy," the larger of the two men tousled his hair with a giant, meaty hand. Alexi smiled and kept moving.

When Alexi reached the raised box framing the cargo hold, he climbed onto it and knelt beside the hatch cover. He pulled with all of his strength, but couldn't budge the heavy wooden grating. He tried for better leverage, but couldn't make it move. Suddenly, two hands lifted him from the hatch cover and set him aside. Alexi turned and found himself facing a mountain of a man. The man had hair as black as coal and a thick bushy beard.

"Try pulling the spike free before you go lifting next time," he said, reaching beneath the far edge of the wooden square. With a yank he pulled out a wooden pin. He tossed the pin to Alexi and walked toward the bow where a group of men were relaxing.

The grate came free easily. Alexi lifted it clear and set it beside the open hole on the hatch cover. He climbed down into the hold, his bag slung over his shoulder.

The hold was dark and smelled of dried fur. As his eyes adjusted to the faint light, bundles of furs appeared all around him. He found the barrels of provisions and filled the bag half full of potatoes and then added some turnips. As he made his way back to the ladder, he noticed barrels of steel tools that were lashed to the sides of the hold. Shovels and axes, rakes and hoes stood tall in their round containers. He was proud, for he knew that his father had made the tools.

He found the ladder and climbed out, careful not to spill his bag as he scrambled onto the deck. Alexi dragged the heavy wooden grate back into place. He replaced the pin then returned to the galley.

"A fine selection lad," the cook voiced his approval. "You are definitely going to be worth the trouble. Now get these cut up, but don't hurry. First dinner isn't until six bells."

"Yes, sir," Alexi smiled back.

"So tell me," Alexi spoke as he selected a sharp knife from the wooden block on the counter, "do your sons hunt and fish?"

"Hah!" The laugh burst from deep in the cook's belly. "Since the day they could fire a musket they have spent half their waking hours prowling the forest. My eldest, Sasha, he's famous for his prowess as a wolf hunter. The winter of his sixteenth year he took three of them on his own. He makes a good living as a hunter and trapper. And Peter, he can fish. He once caught a sturgeon as large as two men. It was the finest tasting fish that ever graced my pan. And the caviar was magnificent," the cook kissed his fingers and rolled his eyes back into his head.

The memories stirred the cook, and he became silent as he thought about his family.

"Only a few short months and I'll be home, leading them around by their ears."

Alexi finished the potatoes and turnips and left the cook the work of making them into a meal. He headed out on deck and leaned against the rail. He looked to the stern deck, the forbidden area, with no great curiosity. Hanging around the shops in New Archangel he had long ago learned that if a craftsman told you not to do something you didn't do it.

A large bundle of sailcloth was lashed against the aft rail, stored there to replace sail damaged by bad weather. He stared into the distance at the shrinking mountains and marveled at their great height. The hills around the fort were no match for these giants. So high were these mountains that the snow still reached far down from the tops in the fading days of summer.

He spent the rest of the day moving between the galley, the rail, and his private spot at the bow. A school of dolphin joined the boat in the late afternoon, riding the wave pushed in front of the ship. They were agile and graceful swimmers.

When the dolphins tired of the ship, he went below to his bunk. He dozed off and was awakened by the sound of the dinner bell. The men who had been sleeping in the foc'sle quickly came to life. Being the last one to dinner meant you might go hungry.

Chapter 6

The third day broke violently. A sour stomach and spinning head greeted Alexi. As consciousness crept into his mind, he felt his small bunk rising and falling a great distance. A wave of sickness flooded over him and he felt he might vomit. As he slipped out of his bunk, he was pushed hard against the edge as the bow headed up a wave. He floated momentarily above the floor as the deck plunged from beneath him. When the ship bottomed in the wave, he was dragged to the floor and struggled to stay on his feet. The ship groaned and creaked.

A panic gripped Alexi and he momentarily forgot his discomfort as he struggled up the ladder and onto the deck. All hands were tending the sails that glowed white against a blackened sky. The sunshine that had greeted him the morning before was only a glow in the east. Holding tight to a safety rope that had been stretched from the foc'sle door to the rail, he made his way across the pitching deck and clung to the rail. He could no longer control his body and he heaved into the churning water and shut his eyes.

The fresh air and spray in his face lifted his spirits, and the sick feeling began to ease. He watched as the men scrambled about the deck, taking their orders from the mate, as the captain himself manned the helm. The wind blew from the south and west and was pushing the *Irena* back toward the coast.

Through the small porthole, Alexi caught a glimpse of the cook. He paused a moment to time the waves then made a quick dash for the galley.

He burst into the galley, slamming the door behind him, falling onto the bench behind the table.

"A fine entrance lad," the cook complimented him from behind a smile.

"How long has the weather been foul?" Alexi asked.

"The captain said just after midnight the wind veered. It must be blowing forty knots. We have lost much of our seaway. The mountains on the coast are growing near again," the cook was suddenly serious. "It will add two or three days to the passage if this wind keeps up."

"There isn't a chance we will run into the coast is there?" Alexi asked his new friend, concern crept into his tone.

"What? No. The captain has things well in hand. We are making way toward Kodiak. Progress comes in baby steps now instead of the great leaps of the past days. Don't you worry lad, this is where a sailor is at his best. You just try to keep my good food where it belongs in the future, eh?" The cook tossed him a wet cloth and indicated he should rub his face with it.

The cloth was warm and smelled of soap. Alexi scrubbed his face and neck. The cook had a way of putting him at ease. His stomach had calmed and he felt good again.

The cook kept Alexi busy with chores through the morning. Preparing a meal in a bobbing galley was not a simple task, but the cook made things look easy. Soon the motion of the boat became second nature to Alexi.

The weather worsened and spray slammed against the galley as waves broke against the side of the *Irena*, but the cook showed little concern.

All day Alexi had been telling the cook of his adventures

in his baidarka around New Archangel and of his encounters with the Kolosh. The cook had listened and had shared a few stories in return. Some were enough to raise hairs on the back of Alexi's neck, and his admiration for his new friend grew with each tale.

In the early afternoon, the cook sprung a surprise on Alexi.

"Alexi, you have performed admirably these past few days. Most boys your age couldn't be counted on to keep their lunch off the deck. I have a special surprise if you can run and fetch it."

"What sort of surprise?" Alexi asked.

"Have you ever eaten a fresh apple?" the cook asked.

"No sir. I once had a slice of apple pie at a dinner at the school," Alexi said.

"Well, then. You *are* in for a treat," the cook smiled broadly. "Down in the hold behind the large keg of potatoes you will find a small wooden crate. The lid is tied in place with heavy twine. Untie the twine and bring out four good apples. The crew can enjoy a few steamed slices with their dinner, and you may have one for yourself."

Alexi's eyes lit up. "I'll be right back," he was turned and almost out the galley door when the cook called sharply to him.

"Mind your step down there. The boat is moving dangerously and things aren't always tightly secured," the cook warned.

The ship was rolling sharply, the deck moved a great deal past level as the boat heeled before the wind and swells.

"I'll be careful," he smiled at the cook, and was gone from the door.

The ocean had turned an angry gray, its surface streaked with long white trails of foam as the crests of the breaking waves were blown away by the wind. A steady rain pelted Alexi's face. The sails were trimmed to carry much less wind. The crew wore grim masks of concentration as they moved in the rigging, adjusting lines and watching the sails for the slightest change that might require their attention.

The swells were steeper than he had ever seen.

Alexi passed unnoticed as he made his way to the wooden grate. He moved in a crouch, keeping his arms outstretched for balance as the boat pitched wildly.

He made it to the hatch and took hold of the grate to maintain his balance. When the ship steadied for a moment, he pulled the wooden pin from its hole and slipped it into his pocket. Using the motion of the boat as a lever, he lifted the heavy wooden grate and slid it aside. The weight of the cover and the rough canvas stretched over the hatch kept the grate from sliding away.

Alexi slipped over the edge and descended into the darkness. He had to strain his eyes and feel his way toward the food barrels. He bounced between the barrels of rattling tools and bundles of fur as he made his way aft. The motion of the boat was not as noticeable deep in the hull and he was able to relax a bit to look for the apples.

He found them quickly and spent a few minutes working on the knots that bound the crate. When he had the crate open, Alexi selected four apples and tucked them into the cloth bag. He re-tied the ropes on the crate and turned to make his way back on deck. As he did, the boat gave a violent groaning lurch, heeling over onto its side. At the same time, a deafening crashing sound drowned out the creaking of the wooden planks and the hold went black.

A bundle of tools broke free of its binding and showered out of the darkness. A large wooden crate hopped from behind a cargo net. The corner of the crate struck Alexi sharply across his temple. Everything went even blacker amid a shower of stars.

Chapter 7

A gray fog rolled across the sound. The loons whistled to one another as Alexi sat in his baidarka, staring out across the great expanse of the sea. The fog lifted quickly, and the small boat was suddenly rocking and pitching wildly. The gray faded to total blackness. The creaking of heavy timbers filled his ears, and the boy felt his body rocking as if in a cradle. His memory flooded back and the boy knew where he was.

A pile of tools pinned Alexi against the bottom of the hold and his head felt as though it had split open. He freed a hand and felt through the tangle of wooden handles and steel points. The smooth outsides of the wooden crate that had struck him in the head sat on top of the jumbled tools. Alexi pushed with all of his strength and the box slid aside. He turned strongly, twisting himself free of the rubble. The boat was rolling wildly, faster and much further than he could remember at any time on the voyage.

He opened his eyes, but could still only see black. Instinct forced him to wave his hand in front of his open eyes. He saw nothing. He struggled to his feet, but immediately lost his balance as his head began to spin. He sagged backwards against a soft bundle of fur. He turned and clung to the fur, burying his head in the short luxurious hair as he tried to gather his thoughts.

Surely the cook would come for him. He had been gone too long and the great crash must have been something very bad. He wondered why the boat pitched so wildly. He tried to remember the way to the ladder. He released his grip on the comforting fur and felt his way. He found a gap in the bundles and used both outstretched hands to move between the rows, testing the deck in front of him with his feet as he inched forward. Finally his foot struck something solid and he stretched out his invisible arm. The ladder greeted his hand. He gripped the rung tightly and began to climb toward to the hatch.

He clung to the ladder like a leech. It seemed the *Irena* was doing her best to shake him loose. When his head bumped against the hatch, he reached to feel the opening to see what was blocking the light. The rough surface of wet sail canvas was cold to his touch. He pushed against the heavy cotton material. A jagged and solid obstacle covered the small opening, it wouldn't budge.

Alexi strained his ears to hear anything above the groaning of the *Irena's* planks. No sounds came from above; no shouting, no footsteps, nothing. Alexi felt fingers of fear pulling at his stomach. He shouted loudly for help. He pounded against the bottom of the hatch. For what seemed hours he shouted, pounded and listened. He made several trips down the narrow ladder to rest. His lungs burned and a hard knot filled his stomach. No one answered, and no one was pounding on the hatch in reply.

Suddenly the boat heeled far beyond its normal rhythm and paused, tossing Alexi against the tools as he tumbled across the hold. The ship hesitated, as if deciding if it was going to come right again or just lie over and give up the fight. Slowly at first, and then with great force, the *Irena* righted herself. The knot in his stomach went rock hard when he felt the sloshing of icy water around his feet. The ship was sinking.

Fear lifted him to his feet and he struggled against his panic to stop and think. Alexi searched among the scattered tools and after a moment rose with the smooth handle of an axe grasped tightly between his hands. He used the axe for support and felt his way forward until he reached the bulkhead that separated the cargo hold from the foc'sle. Bracing himself against a stack of crates still held in place by their webbing, he began to chop blindly into the heavy timbers of the bulkhead.

He labored with the fury of a madman, stopping only to check his progress. At first his work was random, yielding little for his effort, but as he became comfortable with his stroke the effort began to pay off and he soon had cut a hole large enough to put his hand through. He worked for another hour to make the hole large enough to squeeze through. The *Irena* had gone over twice more and the water now washed around his knees. He could hear and feel the sea as it slopped about in the hold with him.

After one final check around the opening for a sharp point that might catch and trap him, he tossed the axe ahead of him then followed it through, spilling headfirst into the foc'sle. The faintest of light came from the skylight.

He found the ladder and climbed to the door. It took all of his strength to push the door open, and when he did, it swung open wildly. The heavy door swung closed immediately, knocking Alexi from the ladder. After climbing to the door a second time Alexi scrambled onto the pitching deck before the door could swing back.

The sight was unbelievable. The main mast had snapped off and crashed down onto the deck. Its broken end had been driven through the front wall of the galley, scattering a maze of tangled ropes and sailcloth. There was no one on the deck. A faint gray light was all that remained of the day and rain blew across the deck in sheets. Alexi's clothes were soaked through in a moment. He looked over the port rail and froze.

Looming in the growing darkness was a line of tree-covered cliffs. Dark rocks towered behind crashing waves that painted the shore with white spray. Alexi strained his eyes to estimate the distance and decided the *Irena* would be on the rocks soon. Turning back to the chaos on the deck, he saw that both of the longboats were missing from their davits. The crew had abandoned ship and had left him behind. His heart fell as he realized he was alone.

He staggered over the ruined rigging to the galley. The door was wedged shut from the weight of the mast pressing against the roof, and would not budge. The portholes were covered by wet sailcloth. Suddenly a loud rumble sounded over the wind and waves and the *Irena* lurched heavily to port. She had grounded. A heavy wave pounded the starboard side of the ship and lifted her over the rocks. She righted herself and bobbed once again in time with the angry waves.

Alexi abandoned his efforts to enter the galley and made his way back to the foc'sle. He slid down the ladder, landing hard at the bottom. It was nearly dark in the cramped cabin. He dashed to his bunk and quickly stuffed his belongings into his bag. He paused when he dug the last items from his bunk. A small knife and a flint and steel were wrapped tightly with the tin of char cloth in an oiled canvas pouch. The pouch was bound with a short piece of twine. These were his survival tools. His father had given them to him when he had first begun to travel the sound in his baidarka.

"You should never be out in the woods without a knife and fire," his father had always counseled.

He knew he would need them soon. He tucked the pouch deep into the pocket of his trousers.

Hanging from a row of pegs beside the ladder was an oilskin coat. His paddle stood behind the coat. Alexi grabbed the coat from the peg and wrapped his bag in the waterproofed coat. He found a piece of cord hanging from a peg and lashed the bundle tightly.

He took his paddle and moved to the ladder. As he stood to climb the ladder, the ship grounded hard at the bottom of its motion and the *Irena* pitched steeply on her side. Alexi crashed down against the side of the foc'sle. His ribs hit the hard edge of a bunk. The ship righted partway but stopped with the decks tilted at a steep angle. Water began to seep into the cabin. Alexi couldn't see where it was coming in, but he could hear the bubbling and slosh as it found the openings in the battered planking.

He felt the handle of the axe bumping against his leg as he rolled over to get to his feet. He grabbed the axe and wedged the handle between the strands of twine that held his belongings together, then pulled himself up the tilted deck.

He caught the bottom rung of the ladder. The ladder now led sideways to the small gray square that marked the door. He took the twine binding his bundle between his teeth, grabbed the paddle in one hand and climbed the ladder. The bobbing of the *Irena* had become less violent, but he could feel the power of each wave as it crashed against the side of the ship.

The faint outline of the cliffs topped by gnarled trees loomed closer than before. Alexi decided that riding out the storm on the grounded ship would be safest. He climbed through the door to cross to the galley. As he crept across the tilted deck, a huge wave crashed over the rail and swept him into the sea.

Chapter 8

The icy water squeezed the air from his lungs and paralyzed his mind as he plunged beneath the surface. The foamy waves tossed him as though he were a rag doll. He clung to the bundle of clothes and his paddle, knowing they would eventually bring him to the surface.

After an eternity, he bobbed to the surface and his head broke free of the water. He gasped for a breath. The water choked him. Before he could satisfy his need for air, a wave broke over his head and he was pushed under. Darkness engulfed him as he struggled to determine which way was up. Again he bobbed to the surface.

His bundle grew heavier and the axe that was still wound in the strings had shifted and felt as though it might slip free. He didn't have time to worry over it as fresh air had once again made itself available. He gulped the air and prepared for the next wave.

The waves came faster and with greater force. The fourth or fifth wave pushed him all of the way to the bottom and his leg slammed against a sharp rock. Pain shot from his toes to his hip and he screamed in his head. When next he popped to the surface he shook his head to clear the water from his eyes and saw a terrifying sight.

Looming overhead were the jagged cliffs he had seen from the deck of the *Irena*. The air shook as the powerful waves pounded against them.

A feeling of hopelessness swept over him. He managed to keep himself upright as the next wave broke over his shoulders. As he shook the foam from his eyes, a dark opening in the face of the cliffs appeared. He grabbed the paddle and tucked it and his bundle under one arm and swam furiously with his free arm, pulling his bundle behind him. The dark opening drew closer as the next wave washed over him, turning him over several times as it rumbled by. The black gap widened and it was eerily calm between the frothing walls of white foam that broke against the cliffs on either side. He sensed the next wave was nearly upon him and gave his greatest effort to swim into the gap as a huge wall of foam engulfed him.

The cold water had drained his energy and he gave up resisting and let the current take him. Hugging his bundle and paddle close to his chest he squeezed his eyes shut.

The water was suddenly still. Millions of tiny bubbles bumped and slipped along his face. He felt the pressure in his ears easing and his head broke the surface. Alexi rolled onto his back and took great slow drinks of air. The surf still thundered around him. He rolled onto his side and strained his eyes to make out his surroundings. It was nearly black now but he could see the outline of a beach. He kicked his weary legs to reach the shore. His boots scraped against the bottom and he kicked harder, gaining traction and driving himself into shallower water. He released the bundle with one hand and reached beneath him, finding the bottom with numb fingers.

Heavy with water he inched into the shallows and crawled on hands and knees over jagged rocks. The barnacles and sharp rocks tore at his hands and shredded the knees of his trousers. He didn't care. He collapsed onto the beach.

The waters of the sound were rippled by a gentle breeze. A lone eagle soared over a shoal of herring, searching for an easy meal. His small skin boat bobbed gently and he felt the sun on his face. The eagle suddenly dove straight at him, coming in fast and circling behind him as it swooped down from the sky.

A stabbing pain in his back jolted Alexi from his dream. Wet clothing and the roaring surf brought him back to reality. He had settled over a sharp stone and it was digging into his ribcage. He rolled away from the rock onto the oilskin bundle that had saved him from drowning. Fighting off pain that made him sick to his stomach, he rose to his feet and stumbled in the dark up the steep beach, dragging his bundle and feeling his way with his free hand. He soon ran headlong into a thicket of alder. He got down on his knees and picked his way blindly through the thicket and into the woods. A soft carpet of moss greeted him and he rolled onto his back and rested.

He knew that he must get out of his wet clothes. He fumbled with the bundle in the dark trying to find the knots that would free his clothes from the oilskin. He trembled and couldn't control his fingers. Alexi screamed. His fingers would not do as he willed. He sagged back into the cold moss and sobbed. He felt the axe handle against his leg and sat up. He pulled the head of the axe free of its lashing and used it on the strings that bound the oilskin. The strings parted and his bag tumbled from inside the waterproof coat.

Alexi tore open his canvas bag and dug out his clothes. It was an ordeal to get out of his wet clothes and pull on the clothes from his bundle.

He shoved his wet clothes into the bag and picked up the oilskin, the axe and his paddle and made his way deeper into the forest, reaching the root mass of a tree. Alexi dropped the bundle of clothes and his tools on the ground and wrapped the oilskin tightly around his shoulders. He pulled the hood up over his head and hunkered down between two huge roots and shook until he fell asleep...

The Island

Chapter 9

A chattering of a squirrel woke Alexi. He shivered uncontrollably. Every part of his body screamed with pain. Through blurry eyes he could see his swollen, bloody hands. Small cuts and scratches covered his knuckles and blood was crusted over several large gashes. He studied himself without moving, focusing on each part of his body to assess the damage. Ever so slowly he began to move his limbs.

Pushing back the oilskin, he sat up and straightened his legs. The knees of his trousers were soaked through with blood. His legs were numb but he could feel the sting of the cuts.

There was enough light to see clearly. Behind him a cliff rose sharply below a knot of gnarled spruce. In front of him the thicket he had crawled through in the dark formed a barrier between the beach and the forest. He reached down and felt his pocket for his knife and fire tools. They were gone! He remembered he had changed his pants.

Alexi sat forward and dug his wet pants out of his bag. The tools were still in the pocket. He opened the pouch and pulled out the knife and squeezed it tightly in his hand. He put his flint between his teeth and held the steel in his free hand. Pushing himself to his feet he hobbled to the base of the spruce he had slept beneath. He slipped the knife into his pocket and examined the trunk of the tree. White stringy moss hung from a tangle of small, dead branches.

He snapped off a handful of the small branches that were draped with stringy moss. He winced as the sharp twigs reopened his wounds. Fighting back tears he gathered a supply of wood.

He carried the tinder to the base of the tree and made a neat pile in between two roots. With shaking hands, he removed a small square of char cloth from the tin and tucked it deep in the center of the pile. Striking the flint against the steel he sent a shower of sparks into the hole. Several unsuccessful tries to light the char cloth frustrated Alexi and he paused to calm himself before he made another attempt.

This time the shower of sparks caught in the square of cloth, and a small red ember came to life. He leaned in close and gently blew on the glowing ember which quickly grew to a small yellow flicker in the tinder. The flames spread through the moss and began to attack the spruce twigs. Small puffs of white smoke rose from the tiny fire and the first wave of warmth issued from the crackling flames. Alexi sagged to the ground and let the heat soak into his face and hands.

The fire grew hotter as he fed it the small pieces of dry spruce. He wrung the water from his wet clothes and spread them on the moss near the fire to dry. When the fire was going well, he finally stopped to take stock of the morning.

The rain had stopped, yet he hadn't noticed. The skies were gray, and the wind had subsided to a gentle breeze and he could see barely a ripple on the water beyond the thicket. Across a narrow channel, Alexi could make out a rocky shoreline. The warmth from the fire was softening his frozen hands and his cuts began to scream for attention.

He cut a strip of cloth from the hem of his shirt and then divided it into equal lengths. He wrapped the strips of cloth around his tattered hands.

Taking the time to warm himself and regain his wits gave his stomach a chance to remember it hadn't been fed. The ache in his belly grew steadily. The fire was in need of more wood and the feeling had returned to his limbs. Alexi tucked the knife into his pocket and put his fire tools under a root. He made his way through the thicket.

The tide was out. The seaweed that covered the rocks formed a green carpet between the gravel beach and the water. Alexi had landed on the protected shore of a small island. A stone's throw across a channel was another small island. A pair of high cliffs faced each other across the channel. The black hole into which he had plunged the night before was the gap between the islands.

A jagged, brown object caught his eye. A large timber had washed ashore, part of the *Irena*. It had followed him into the channel and bobbed gently in the shallow water against the barnacle-covered rocks.

The timber looked as though it would bear his weight if he floated on it. The opening between the islands was calm. The gentle swells lapped at the rocky cliff.

He returned to the forest and retrieved his paddle. He carried it down to the timber and stepped into the cold water. His feet ached and were tender inside of his boots. He pushed the timber into deeper water and straddled it. One end was neatly trimmed; the other end was a splintered mess. The timber carried him so only his legs were under water. He lay on the timber and paddled toward the gap between the cliffs, the cold water eased the pain in his hands and legs.

He covered the distance to the gap quickly and slid

beyond the cliffs. The vision that greeted him was heart breaking. The battered remains of the *Irena* were stranded on the rocks.

The water between the cliffs and the wreck was calm, interrupted only by a few scattered rocks which were surrounded by rafts of kelp. Jagged rocks topped by gnarled spruce lined the shore as far as he could see in either direction.

The wreck would not be easily located from the sea. His anger flared. How could the crew have abandoned him? His friend the cook was to look out for him. Was the cook's desire to see his family so strong that he would leave his charge to the sea? He couldn't believe that about the man of whom he had grown so fond. Tears welled in his eyes. Where was the crew now? Had they made for home, or had they attempted a landing on the coast?

This was the land of the Kolosh. Several times hunting parties and ships had been forced ashore by storms, and many of them had met their deaths at the hands of the Kolosh. No one would land here deliberately.

The rugged shoreline and the surf would have destroyed the launches in a moment. He decided they would have made for the open sea, ridden out the storm and then set sail for New Archangel. He doubted that any rescue would be sent for *him*, but the fur in the broken ship was worth a fortune. The company would not let it go to waste. He would wait for them to return for the furs and make his safe passage home.

The beam carried him well and he made good progress. As he approached the ship, he could see much of the cargo floating in the water. Several barrels bobbed near the ship, tangled in the mass of sailcloth and rigging lines which hung from the broken mast.

The hull had broken in two places and the bow had rolled

forward on its sprit. The foc'sle, where he had spent his first nights at sea, faced skyward, its innards exposed. The center section was intact but was leaning badly on its side. The mast that had barred his escape from the hold had fallen away and floated beside the half-submerged hatch. The stern section had settled back on the rudder and stood neatly upright. The small cabin that housed the galley and captain's quarters was visible on the after deck. The gaping hole beneath the crushed roof was a gruesome reminder of the *Irena*'s misfortune.

Alexi inspected the floating debris piece by piece. He would need the food to survive until the search party returned. He gathered a length of rope and cut it free from the tangle. He paddled in circles, tying five barrels together into a makeshift raft. Two bore markings he could read, pork and potatoes. The other three were heavy but he could not make out the markings. Alexi made the free end of the rope fast to the back of the beam and began to paddle back toward the gap in the rocks.

He paddled gently at first, trying to conserve his energy, but little seemed to happen. He increased the power of his strokes and slowly began to make progress. His hunger was causing him agony when he finally reached the gap in the cliffs. He rested for several minutes, fighting back tears from the pain and hunger. The barrels in tow began to catch him so he pressed on.

Finally, he hauled up on the beach in front of his camp and pulled the raft of barrels into shallow water. He hadn't the strength to drag the barrels to the tree line, so he retrieved the axe. Two quick strokes opened the top of the pork barrel and he reached in for a handful of salted meat. He wolfed down large mouthfuls of the stringy meat, his eyes watering with satisfaction. He cracked each of the other barrels. In the last was mix of vegetables. He polished off a handful of carrots and a raw potato without stopping and then sat on the shore, his supplies pulled just beyond the water's reach. The hunger that had tormented him gave way to an uncomfortable fullness. He rested his head on his knees, closed his eyes and dozed.

Chapter 10

Cold water lapping at his ankles stirred Alexi from his nap. The tide had risen several feet and his food barrels were floating again. Water had filled the potato keg and a few of the potatoes had spilled from the barrel. He struggled to his feet and gathered them into their container. He dragged the barrels as far up the shore as he could manage and stretched the rope to the alder thicket. He bent down a thick alder and tied the loose end of the rope around the limb. The tension in the small tree would pull the barrels closer to shore as the tide rose.

His meal had filled his stomach, but a powerful thirst consumed him. He wandered along the shore in search of water. He found a small pool in the rocks near the edge of the alders. It was too far from the sea to be a tide pool, and he bent to his knees to test it. The pain of kneeling was too much to bear so he lay on his stomach. The water was fresh and cool. He gulped handful after handful.

Watered and fed, he resumed the salvage of the *Irena*. If the crew returned for the cargo, he would have to save it from being lost in the next storm. He pushed the timber into the water, straddled it and paddled through the opening in the cliffs. The ocean was a glassy calm. He covered the distance to the *Irena* more quickly on the second trip and decided to board the ship to retrieve what he could from her cargo hold.

He tied the timber to a loose line and climbed into the partly submerged cargo hatch. The light illuminated the tilted hold, revealing a jumble of netting and floating cargo. The furs caught his eyes first. Bundles floated free in the large compartment. The silky fur of the pelts was matted and shimmered in the pale light. Alexi swam to the nearest bundle.

He gathered the furs into an orderly group and tied them together. When the fur was secured in a neat raft, he searched for tools. He had to dive to the bottom of the hold to locate the heavy items. He managed to rescue two more axes and two shovels. He lashed the tools on the raft of soggy fur.

Another object caught his attention. Floating in the back corner of the hold was the crate of apples. He waded across and gathered the crate and a keg of black powder that floated nearby. He dragged his prizes to the raft and lashed them to the bundle. Alexi paddled hard for the cliffs. Progress was much slower with the soggy fur, and it took what seemed hours to make any progress. Exhausted to the point of being sick, he paused in the gap to rest. As he dozed on the beam, Alexi dreamed of paddling his baidarka among the islands of the sound.

He made it to shore and took only enough time to pull the bundles clear of the water's reach. He cut the string that bound the box of apples and plucked a piece of the red fruit from under the lid. He bit off a large chunk and chewed it noisily, smiling. The bite of the fruit that had led to his being stranded filled his mouth with pleasure. The sweet juices ran from the corner of his mouth as the crisp flesh crunched between his teeth. He devoured the apple in six bites before replacing the lid and carrying the crate to the alder thicket. He returned for the keg of powder and lashed the bundles of fur to an alder.

The chill was gone from the air and a warm breeze began to blow from the south. The sunshine on his back warmed him. He decided to build up his strength before attempting another trip to the ship so he abandoned the cargo and headed back to the woods.

The coals from the fire were cold but dry. He gathered moss and spruce branches. The cloth wrapped around his hands offered protection from the rough job and he wished he had thought of it the night before.

He managed to coax a fire from the pile of tinder with just three strikes of his flint and steel. He warmed himself, savoring the heat. He left the fire long enough to retrieve the case of apples and took a second piece of fruit. He ate slowly, savoring each bite and let the sweetness linger on his tongue. Warmed but not dry, Alexi headed back to the beach.

Reluctantly he pushed the beam into deeper water and shuddered as the cold water once again soaked him to his waist. He had mastered paddling the beam and was soon nearing the wreck. He paused about twenty yards from the broken hulk and bobbed gently in the calm sea. Such a great ship the *Irena* had been. How sad that she had ended on this barren shore.

He tied the beam and made his way through the hold into the lower deck of the stern section. The bottom of the hull was full of splintered holes. Water flowed waist deep as he felt his way toward the ladder to the captain's stateroom on the middle deck.

The ladder was intact and he had only to push the hatch cover gently aside to enter the tiny cabin. The captain's quarters were located beneath the galley. The stateroom was amazingly intact. Glasses and the captain's books, which had flown from their shelves when the ship had grounded, lay scattered on the floor. The thick glass windows cut into the stern of the ship let in ample light.

A spyglass lay beside a stack of seaman's books near an overturned table. He picked it up and tried it. The lens was broken. He placed the polished brass tube back on the floor. He moved toward a locker that reached from floor to ceiling. The door hasp was pinned shut with a tiny ivory marlinspike hung from a twine.

He pulled the pin and opened the locker. Two beautiful long guns stood side by side in the cupboard. A shelf above the long guns held several bags of shot, patches and a powder horn. A brass compass sat on the left side of the shelf. Alexi pocketed the compass and then removed the firearms and hefted them one at a time. They were identical and bore no distinguishing markings beside the gunsmith's signature. He pointed the long guns around the cabin, steadying them on the light from the windows and squeezing gently on the triggers.

The long guns would be important to his survival. He stood the long guns in the corner near the ladder and stacked the shooting supplies beside them.

His search of the captain's cabin complete, Alexi climbed another ladder to the hatch in the main deck behind the galley. The hatch was stuck and he had to press his shoulder hard against it before it gave. The hatch flew open slamming on the deck above. The sound scared him. The abandoned ship was so silent. He pulled himself through the hatch and stood on the deck. The view was magnificent. The rocky shoreline stretched as far as he could see in both directions, fading gradually to a white line of horizon. The wind was picking up. A light chop stirred the tops of the gentle swells. The sun still shone brightly across the blue water, but clouds were gathering in the south.

Alexi turned his attention to the shattered cabin that had once been the galley. The rear of the small cabin was the only part intact. The door stood open, swinging gently in the breeze, inviting him in. He approached the door slowly, unsure of what he might find. The inside of the cabin was shadowed, light filtered in through gaps in the broken roof and the gaping hole in the forward bulkhead.

It was as if someone had taken the galley and shaken it upside down. The pots, pans, dishes and silverware that had been neatly stowed were spread rumble tumble about the cabin. The table had been torn from its pedestal and stood balanced on edge between the bench and counter. Pieces of planking and timbers torn from overhead were mixed in with the cooking gear. As his eyes adjusted he moved into the cabin, inching forward.

Something beneath the broken table caught his eye. A white apron tail lay draped over a pile of rubble. Alexi moved closer. His heart stopped. Beneath the crumpled apron the outline of a leg took shape. He took hold of the edge of the table, frozen for a moment with dread. He gave a strong pull on the tilted table and it fell toward him, crashing loudly onto the littered floor.

There lay his friend, the cook. Alexi stared, rooted in place, his breath caught in his lungs. The cook's apron was stained deep red over his chest. His face was as white as a peeled potato, his lips an unnatural gray. The cook's eyes were closed, but his face looked pained.

Alexi knew why he had been left in the Hold. He sank to his knees. Tears welled in his eyes and he buried his face in his hands and sobbed. His friend would never see his sons, his wife or his farm, and Alexi would never hear another of his wonderful stories.

Finally Alexi dried his eyes and got to his feet. The light

was fading and Alexi decided to make for camp. He selected a pair of iron pots, a pewter mug and a large wooden spoon from the floor near the door and left the crushed cabin.

Alexi retraced his steps to the captain's cabin and collected the long guns and shooting supplies. It took three trips to get his collection secured to the beam. The swells were growing as he paddled toward the gap in the cliffs. The clouds had overtaken the sun and the air was cool. He was numb from the cold, but the sadness he felt from the discovery of his dead friend pushed the discomfort from his mind.

He covered the distance to his camp easily and pulled the wooden beam as far up on the shore as he was able. He lashed it to the base of an alder, untied his prizes and headed back to rekindle his fire.

Chapter 11

The coals were still warm and he managed to revive the flames by gently blowing on them beneath a pile of fresh moss and twigs. The fire buoyed his spirits and he fed it larger sticks until a pleasant blaze danced between the roots. His clothes were mostly dry so he slipped from his wet garments and pulled on dry pants and jersey. The clothes felt like a warm blanket on a cold night. The constant exposure to seawater had left him waterlogged. His fingers were wrinkled and puffy and the cloth strips he had wrapped around his hands were soaked through with fresh blood.

He gently unwound his bandages and examined the damage. Dozens of small scratches crisscrossed the palms of each hand, but there were only a few deep cuts. None of them would trouble him beyond a few days. After he had soaked up enough heat from the fire, he headed back to the beach for some potatoes and meat.

He filled the small pot with water from the pool and boiled potatoes and salt pork in the coals of the fire. He burned his mouth as he devoured the steaming meal. He drank the broth from the pot and lay back on the soft moss. Though his body was telling him to close his eyes, he forced himself to his feet and shook off the urge to sleep.

He walked through the thicket and took stock of the rescued cargo. The bundles of fur and barrels were stranded on the rocky shore by the falling tide. He set about moving everything above the reach of the next tide. He rolled the barrels carefully over the jagged rocks until they were tucked under the curve of the alder thicket. He cut the bundles of furs apart and carried them in small loads inside the edge of the thicket.

The thin alders in the thicket grew too close together to allow for the passage of an item of great size. Alexi used his axe to clear a trail wide enough for him to carry a bundle of furs. When the light was nearly gone, he returned to his fire. Tomorrow he would gather in a supply of wood and build a shelter. His body ached as never before.

He spread his wet clothes over low branches near the fire to dry. If rain came in the night his clothes would get no wetter. A patch of sailcloth he had spread with his clothes had dried well during the day, and he tucked it inside of the oil skin and pulled them both around his shoulders and sat down by his fire. He leaned back against the roots of the spruce and closed his eyes.

The boy was poking a long stick into holes along the shore. He carried a wooden bowl in his hand, moving carefully so as not to spill its contents. He paused in front of a hole at the base of a large rock near the lowest reach of the slimy green beach. He poked gently into the hole with the stick and then moved back and set the stick down. He returned with the bowl cradled gently between his hands. Kneeling, he reached his hands into the small hole and emptied the bowl. He moved back and stood to the side of the rock.

Several minutes passed and still the boy waited. Slowly a thin, black tendril wriggled out from the darkness of the hole, testing the rocks and grasses. Soon a second finger-like tentacle joined the first. The arms grew longer and the suckers lining the bottom of each arm became visible. Sensing it was safe, the octopus began to follow its sensing tips from under the rock. The boy waited. When the entire creature had emerged and was moving toward the water, the boy leapt from behind the rock and pounced. The octopus was no match and the boy ran screaming down the beach, carrying his prize. A group of women gathered on the beach far in the distance clapped loudly, shouting encouragement in their strange tongue.

Alexi snapped from his dream, a corner of the sailcloth flapped against his ear. The wind had returned. Alexi sat upright, his muscles protested the sudden movement.

The wind was blowing from the shore, coming directly into his camp, stirring the clothes on the bushes surrounding his dead fire. It was cold. The early morning sky was a dark gray blanket.

He shrugged off the sailcloth and oilskin and stretched slowly to standing. His feet hurt badly and a sudden wave of sickness wrenched his stomach. He fought off the feeling and forced himself to hobble to the beach. The tide was high and his beam bumped against the shore, pushed by the breeze. He walked to the point that offered a view of the open sea through the gap in the cliffs.

The sight that greeted him stirred him to action. The water was churning again, though now the waves were not coming directly onshore. The wind that seemed to be coming from the shore was actually moving from the south and pushing waves across the shoals. The bow of the *Irena* had rolled onto its top. The curved keel knifed into the air, the foc'sle facing north as the remnants of the cabin bobbed in the surf. It had come off of the rocks and was beginning to move. The high tide and increasing wind might shift the entire ship before he could finish his salvage.

He walked back to his camp and dug a handful of carrots from a barrel. The carrots were crisp and he savored their sweet flavor. After his breakfast, he walked to the small pool and drank mightily of the fresh water. He went back to his camp and changed into his wet clothes. He would save his dry clothes for when he returned and was frozen. The chill of the wet clothes was almost unbearable, but the need to finish his work aboard the *Irena* moved him to action in spite of his misery.

He wrapped his dry clothing in the section of sailcloth and the oilskin and tucked the bundle beneath a spruce tree near the fire.

The icy water wasn't much of a shock after the soaked clothes. He was becoming used to it. He pushed the beam off of the shore and headed to the wreck. The wind hit him hard as he cleared the cliffs. The waves weren't as large as the night he had been marooned, but they were formidable. Walls of white crashed over the exposed rocks that dotted the shoreline, leaving patches of floating foam in their place. They crashed against the stern of the *Irena*. Alexi could see the ship's hull moving under the pressure.

The waves broke over the beam, nearly unseating Alexi many times. He squeezed tightly with his knees. Twice he was turned sideways by the force of the waves, but each time managed to bring the beam into the sea and again make headway. His strength was fading when he reached the shelter of the open hatch. He slipped from the beam and made it fast to a broken plank.

The water was deeper in the hold, and he had to swim to the ladder. Alexi rested at the bottom of the ladder. He could feel the ship move under the force of the waves. It shifted slightly with each collision and he knew he had less time than he had hoped.

The ladder was easy to climb with empty hands. He paused at the top of the ladder, reminding himself of the grave task ahead. His friend lay in the broken cabin. Though he had known the cook for only a few days, the man had shown him great kindness and treated him as a man and not a boy. Alexi intended that his friend receive the best treatment in death that he could provide.

He mustered his courage and marched into the cabin. The warmth of the fire and the aroma of the cook's meals were gone. The smell of spoiled food had begun to mingle with the salt air. Alexi went back on deck and found a length of heavy rope dangling over the rail. He cut the line free with his knife and coiled it over his shoulder.

Returning to the galley, he fashioned a small loop in one end of the line. He knelt beside the battered body of his friend. Again, tears filled his eyes, and he had to wipe them away with his sleeve. He slipped the loop over the cook's pink scalp and ears, gently lifting the cook's head from the floor. One arm at a time, he pulled the cook's stiff limbs through the loop, and worked the rope behind the cook's shoulders under his arms. Alexi stepped back and pulled the slack from the rope. The loop tightened and dug into the cook's fleshy sides. Alexi winced as he wiped tears from his eyes. There should be strong men here to lift this kind soul and carry him with dignity to his resting-place.

No one would step forward to help him. He pulled, closing his eyes against the sight, and felt the cook's body slide toward him on the wooden floor. Slowly and in small movements, he dragged the heavy man toward the doorway.

As he struggled to move the heavy body, he thought of a way to make the task easier. He untied the loop from around the cook and dropped the line beside the body. He hurried out of the cabin to the stern rail. The large bundle of sailcloth that was lashed to the rail would make a perfect shroud. He slit the lashings on the bundle of cloth. The cloth hung in place for a moment, stiffened by long holding its position. Gradually, the bundle of white cloth tumbled forward, spilling against Alexi's feet.

Alexi's heart stopped momentarily. His tears froze in their ducts and his breath left him as if a great weight had been dropped on his chest. Behind the folded canvas lay his baidarka. The surprise his father had promised was revealed.

When his heart resumed beating and he could again draw a breath, he leaned close and ran his hand over the tight skin of his baidarka. This was the greatest gift he could ever have dreamed of. His woven grass mat was neatly folded in the bow and the seal intestine coat used for protection from the rain and spray was folded beneath it. Alexi jumped with joy.

Chapter 12

The task of wrapping the cook's body and getting it to shore pushed to the front of Alexi's mind and he turned from his prize. He dragged the canvas to the galley and spread the cloth over the floor beside the cook. He cut the extra cloth away and rolled the cook until he lay face up in the middle of the cloth. Alexi wrapped the extra cloth over the cook's body completely sealing him inside the white canvas.

Alexi felt a wave of relief. He cut several lengths of line and tied the shroud at the cook's knees, waist and shoulders. Pulling on the loop of line around the cook's knees, he was able to drag the bundle to the edge of the deck.

He was pondering how he might lower the body into the water when a huge wave crashed against the stern. The ship pitched forward, spilling the shrouded body and Alexi into the water. Alexi struggled to the surface in the shadow of the ship. He righted himself and took a deep breath. The body floated beside him and he took hold of the line and made it fast to a broken plank. The hull of the *Irena* loomed over him.

His baidarka awaited rescue and Alexi swam back to the ladder. The hull was tilted forward at such an angle that the ladder stretched back over his head. He climbed hand over hand up the slanting ladder and scrambled through the floor of the captain's cabin. Repeating the process for the second ladder, he found himself hanging at his waist through the hatch in the aft deck.

His baidarka lay against the back of the cabin. Slipping his feet over the lip of the hatch he held onto it tightly and let his feet slide slowly towards his baidarka. He let go his grip on the hatch and slid the last bit, coming to rest on the back of the galley cabin. He pulled his baidarka over his shoulder. Inching along the cabin, he made his way to its edge.

The deck was tilted at such a steep angle that he feared that he would slide into the water. A fall could break the skin covering. He cut a length of line and fastened it around the bow of the baidarka. Holding the line he made a short leap to the rail and wrapped his legs around it.

Pulling on the lanyard, he slowly worked the boat to the rail. When he had the bow securely in his grip, he pulled the boat bit by bit across his body until it balanced on the railing. The water was churning violently. Holding tightly to the lanyard, he lowered his boat to the water.

The baidarka settled stern first in the water, then righted itself and bobbed at ease. He secured the line around his waist and slid down the wet planking. He fell the final distance into the water, landing on his back.

He swam to the beam, towing the baidarka. He retrieved his paddle and slid it into the cockpit of the baidarka. Maneuvering himself to the stern of the skin boat, he grabbed the edge of the cockpit with both hands and with a great pull, slid up the back deck and came to rest astride the baidarka with his legs behind the opening. He balanced there for a moment, regaining his feel for the boat. With a second effort he pulled his legs around, pointed them forward and dropped his rear through the hole. Tucking his knees tightly to his chest, he slipped his feet, ankles and then knees beneath the forward deck of the baidarka.

He felt the paddle against his thigh and pulled it out and dipped it lightly on both sides of the boat. He could hear the ship groan as the waves pushed harder. He spun the baidarka around and paddled between the broken sections of the ship. The cook's body bobbed in the water, the air trapped in the canvas giving it buoyancy. Alexi cut the body free from the broken plank and tied the lanyard around his waist. Pulling on his paddle, he turned and made for the gap between the cliffs.

The waves lifted him high and he paddled furiously to make headway, dragging the heavy bundle behind him while he fought the wind and seas. The baidarka was much more nimble than the beam and he reached the cliffs easily. A large wave picked him up as he entered the gap and he brushed against the rocky cliff. The baidarka shot through the last stretch and Alexi was in the protected channel behind his island. He beached his baidarka and pulled the cook's body up on the shore and sat down to rest.

Rain rattled on the baidarka. The drops were comforting as they struck his face. The cold water had numbed him but his face welcomed the shower. Heavy gusts tore at the trees on the shore across the inlet. The storm grew angrier each moment. He had to move his friend's body above the reach of the tide.

Struggling against the protests of stiff limbs he carried the baidarka to the edge of the alders. He returned and made his best effort to pull the water-soaked shroud clear of the water.

It was of no use. Weakened, he was unable to budge the cook's body. The tears came again. He sucked in heaving gasps and sat back on the slippery green seaweed and hung his head between his knees. The wind gnawed at the edges of his wet clothing. Chills ran over his body and he began shaking uncontrollably. He needed to get warm. He grabbed the line and stumbled toward the alders. When he reached the end of the rope, he lay it down and made his way to the edge of the thicket.

The shaking made it difficult to pick up the rope that had secured the furs. He joined the two ropes to keep the body from drifting away.

The chore finished, he lumbered over his rough trail and fell to his knees at the base of the spruce. He gasped between chattering teeth as he collected moss and spruce twigs.

He struggled to break the smallest of branches and felt his mind begin to wander. The small pile of tinder with a square of char cloth tucked deep inside resisted his clumsy efforts with flint and steel. He shouted aloud his frustration as he could not make a spark stick on the square of black cloth. He rolled onto his back and squeezed his eyes shut, trying to calm his shaking hands and collect his thoughts. Suddenly he remembered the powder horn. He rolled over and scrambled to the bottom of the spruce where he had stored the shooting supplies and pulled the powder horn out and crawled back to the fire. He poured a healthy measure of the shiny black powder onto the tinder pile and set the powder horn aside. It took but a single spark to ignite the pile of powder and the powder and pile of tinder quickly burst into to a small flame with a large flash of smoke. Alexi hastily stacked fuel on the tiny flame and it grew brighter. Moving close to the flames, heat began to warm his face and hands, slowly penetrating the numbness. He curled around the fire pit, feeding the flames while the warmth soaked into his body.

His stomach reminded him that it had been ignored, a sign that he had warmed enough. The rain began to shower down in large drops. The wind shook the branches and the sky darkened. Alexi chewed a handful of carrots and some cold pork as he huddled under the oilskin.

Following his meal he put his axe to work and gathered a supply of larger branches. The fire crackled and popped, sending showers of sparks soaring high into the soggy branches above him. The storm raged as he sat wedged against the spruce. Alexi used his knife to carve two notches in a large root, one for each day he had spent on the island. The howling wind and roar of the surf pounding on rocky shores lulled him to sleep.

Chapter 13

Dawn crept in, cold and gray. Alexi was painfully hungry. He crawled, shivering, from under his tarp and examined his fire. The ashes were a chalky black sludge. He knelt and put his hand over the coals. They were still very warm so he gathered a few small branches. He stirred the coals, bringing those deep in the pile to the surface. A faint yellow glow emanated from the exposed embers and he placed the handful of tinder over the remains. Bending close, he blew gently at the base of the pile and nursed the coals to life. Flames spread quickly and his fire was reborn. He stoked it with larger branches and lingered, unwilling to move to the tasks that waited.

He opened the crate of apples. The first piece of fruit that met his hand became breakfast. He devoured the apple as he sat wrapped in his tarp beside his fire.

When he could delay no longer, Alexi pulled on his canvas jacket and hobbled to the shore. The tide was receding, and though the rain stung his face, he could make out the white bundle stranded high on the shore near the trail. With his strength renewed, Alexi tried to drag the body higher up on the shore. But try as he might he made no progress.

He returned to the fire and decided to stay close to camp until the tide returned and then he would bury his friend. He dozed fitfully through the day, waking occasionally to stoke his fire and check the tide.

By late afternoon the wind weakened, and the rain no longer blew past in sheets. Alexi spread his oilskin on the ground beside the fire to dry and returned to the beach carrying a shovel. The water was within a foot of the cook's body.

He wedged the handle of the shovel under the middle of the body. The added leverage was all that he needed, and the body rolled toward him into the water. He undid the knot that joined the two lines and floated the body along the shore, away from his camp.

Half a league down the shore, he reached a short patch of beach covered with small stones. He rolled the cook up the gentle slope of the beach until he rested beside the grass below the alder thicket. He began to dig. The shovel reopened the wounds on his hands and the blood made the handle slick. He had to rinse his hands several times during the digging.

Satisfied with the hole he had dug, he moved on to the task he most dreaded. Kneeling beside his friend's body, he slowly undid the bindings. He unfolded the ends of the bundle and pulled open the shroud. He rolled the body over to finish the unwrapping, and found himself staring into an unrecognizable face. A silver medallion hung from the cook's neck, dangling beside his ear. Alexi cut the leather cord with his knife and tucked the silver disk into his pocket. Alexi removed the cook's pocket watch from the cook's soggy shirt. He tucked the watch into his pocket and re-wrapped the body. A more hideous sight he had never seen, and it pained him to know that just a few short days ago the cold swollen corpse had been a vibrant man.

The cook was with God. Father Nikolai's teachings left him confident of that. He worked the body into the shallow grave then gently placed shovels of gravel over the shroud until it was completely covered. Alexi brought larger stones from the water's edge and stacked them over the grave. The pile reached to his knees.

His arms ached and his hands stung. He soaked the blood and dirt from cuts and blisters in seawater.

He sat back on the wet ground and pulled the watch and medallion from his pocket. The gold inside the cover of the watch still glowed with the magic yellow of fire. The watch had stopped working and water dripped from the stem. He read the inscription again, realizing he had never asked the cook his name.

"I promise you, I will return this watch to your family and tell them of the last days of your great life," Alexi said aloud. He placed the items in his pocket and walked back to his camp.

He spent the remainder of the day organizing his supplies. He sorted the food stores and covered them with a canvas. He dragged the damp bundles of fur up the hill behind his campsite and hung them from branches with short strands of rope. He selected a dozen of the driest pelts to line his bed. Although the rain would wet the hanging furs, it would also rinse the salt from the pelts. When the weather broke he would use fresh water to rinse them properly.

He stretched the square of sailcloth between the large spruce and the branches of nearby trees forming a cover from the rain. As evening approached, the wind increased suddenly and he abandoned his work. He wrapped himself in pelts under the oilskin and slept soundly.

The storm raged for three days. Alexi used the time to rebuild his strength, sleeping for long periods. He rose a few times each day to eat and drink and stretch his muscles.

The rain fell in sheets beyond the alders, but the thick

boughs of the spruce and his canvas tarp kept him dry.

On the morning after the storm, Alexi awoke very early. Light flooded in through the trees. The air had warmed and a heavy fog hung over the water. He could barely see the beach. Alexi felt rested and was excited to see what the day might bring.

The forest and seashore smelled wonderful and he drew their aromas deep into his lungs. Alexi savored them one at a time as he sorted the familiar scents in his mind. He could taste the thick moss, musty with the smell of the fine black soil beneath its thin roots. The sticky scent of spruce pitch spread on the gentle breeze. The sweetness of the green kelp that littered the shoreline drifted through his mind next.

He imagined himself sitting on his favorite rock on the shore in New Archangel, eyes closed, listening to the seabirds as they went about finding a meal of fish.

He strolled to the water's edge. His baidarka was tucked under the edge of the alders. The sun faintly shone on it and a fine mist rose from the skin. It would soon dry and tighten over the spruce framework. The ocean was quiet.

Alexi walked to the grave. The storm hadn't disturbed the burial mound, and he felt confident that it would last. The sadness for the loss of his friend was still there, but tears stayed away.

Chapter 14

After a breakfast of apples and carrots, Alexi washed himself in the pool beside the alders and built a small fire. The day would be sunny and warm and he would take advantage of the break to dry his belongings. As he warmed himself by the fire, he spread his canvas tarp and damp clothes over the branches around the fire. He gathered soft branch tips from hemlock trees and spread them on the ground under his tarp. They would provide a soft mattress between his sleeping roll and the cold ground.

With his stomach full, he decided to explore. He collected his fire starting tools and knife. He cut a square of sailcloth and wrapped up several carrots, a turnip and a small piece of salted pork, binding it with a length of line. He pulled the axe from the root of a spruce and carried it to the shoreline. He stopped at the small pool and drank deeply.

Alexi left his axe and lunch at the water's edge and retrieved his baidarka. The boat felt good on his shoulder. He would, after all, have a good friend to keep him company. He lowered the baidarka into the water and tucked the axe and his lunch under the back deck. He pulled the intestine coat from under the bow and slipped it over his shirt. The baidarka rocked a few times as he settled onto the grass mat, but soon steadied itself.

He decided first to see how the *Irena* had weathered the storm, and he nosed the baidarka toward the gap in the cliffs.

The water was glassy with a gentle swell. With no burden towing behind, the boat was as nimble as a swallow. He glided smoothly between the cliffs.

The *Irena* had vanished.

He scanned the shoreline for signs of the hull but saw nothing but ragged breakers trailing off into the distance. He was stunned. The force of the storm must have been awesome, and he suddenly lost hope of rescue. He had counted on the wreck to serve as a beacon, that here *he* was.

Alexi drifted silently, the effect of the ship's disappearance sinking in. He had survived the wreck. He had rescued his friend and seen to his burial. He had salvaged the pelts and a supply of food. Most importantly, he had his baidarka.

He could hunt, fish, forage for food along the coastline and when the time came, he could make his way home to New Archangel.

Recounting all that he had accomplished made him proud, and he decided not to dwell on loss of the wreck. He estimated the launches from the *Irena* might reach New Archangel in two weeks. It might take a month for them to return for her cargo. He would have a good deal of time to fill, and it would require resources beyond what filled the barrels and boxes in his camp.

Alexi swung the bow of the small boat back toward the gap in the cliffs. He would explore to the south of his camp. He set out slowly down the channel that separated his island from the shore. The south end of the island narrowed to a thin peninsula fifty paces beyond the grave. He could see the mound of stones clearly.

The shore of the mainland was rocky and jagged, with few gentle beaches on which to land a boat. Alexi picked his way along the coast between the large rocks and small islands. Thick rafts of kelp surrounded the rocks. Beyond the kelp the water was deep enough for a large vessel to navigate. He decided to poke his nose out onto the ocean.

He angled the baidarka to the west and slipped between two large rocks, nudging the kelp. He had counted islands as he had traveled south and knew he would have to pass seven to return to his camp.

Alexi focused on his strokes, making them even and steady and was soon far from shore.

When the muscles in his shoulders began to protest, he slowed and dragged his paddle against the stern. The baidarka cut a gentle arc, coming full around. Alabaster peaks, jagged and imposing, dwarfed the low mountains along the coast. Long blue shadows filled the valleys between the peaks. Glaciers, too numerous to be counted, clung to the steep slopes. The mountains stretched as far as he could see to the west. To the southeast, in the direction of New Archangel, the mountains became less magnificent as they trailed off into the distance.

Alexi picked out the tallest peak. He wished to mark his island from the sea on the chance that he might someday have to return, so he paddled slowly northwest along the coastline, studying the tall mountains and rolling hills. Hunger tugged at his stomach and he decided to have lunch. He retrieved the canvas pouch and spread his lunch between his knees in the bottom of the baidarka. He finished the carrots, the turnip and the small piece of meat, savoring each bite and enjoying the warmth of the sun.

Flocks of seabirds worked schools of small fish that moved around him as though he were invisible. The screeching and chatter of the gulls and the clucking of the surf ducks brought the sound to mind. He continued paralleling the shore as he counted the islands. Soon he could make out the gap between the cliffs that marked his camp. He coasted to a stop and stared at the shoreline.

Far in the distance, the jagged peak of the tallest mountain towered above the gap in the cliffs. A rounded mountain on the shore behind his island was in line with the big mountain. Near the crest of its rounded top, a blaze of white rock cut across the green hillside. The peak and the blaze lined up perfectly to mark the entrance to his lagoon. He fished the compass from his pocket and took a bearing. Thirty-seven degrees north-northeast gave him a direct line to the mountain peak. Satisfied with his discoveries, he made his way toward the gap in the cliffs.

Alexi shed his thin coat when he reached his island and spent the afternoon cutting limbs from the trees behind his camp. He dragged the boughs back to camp and trimmed the branches. He used the branches to build and thatch a small shelter.

He dug the long guns, the powder and the shot from under the pile of canvas and moved them to the shelter. They would stay dry until he could test them.

By the time he sat down for a rest, the sun had almost dipped below the horizon. The shadows grew long and the air cooled.

By morning, gray skies had returned. The air was chill and Alexi warmed himself as he stirred the coals to life again. An apple, carrots and a small piece of pork were breakfast. As he ate, he recalled the many things the sea and forest offered for food. Tradesmen had little time for fishing and gathering food, so most of what Alexi knew came from his own experiences. He had watched the Kolosh forage among the rocks for their food and knew that the crab hid in grasses in shallow water near the shore. He set out to see what he might find.

He cut a straight limb from an alder and peeled the bark with his knife. The stick was two fingers thick and slightly higher than his head. He sharpened one end to a point and cut a pair of barbs behind the point. It would make a fine spear.

Alexi lashed the spear to the side of his baidarka and set out following the shoreline to the north. He watched the bottom as he paddled through the calm water. Flounders scattered below him as he inched his way along.

He hadn't gone far when an orange shape darted between tufts of grass; a crab. He gave a few gentle strokes and followed. The crab appeared directly under his port side. He untied his spear and pinned the scrambling creature against the bottom. When he was satisfied that the crab had died, he dragged it to the surface.

He slid the lance back through his hands, plucked the skewered crab from the end and paddled back to camp.

The pot of water boiled over a bed of hot coals, and the crab was soon ready. Alexi tore the shell from the crab's body and pulled the legs off one at a time, cracking open the shell to get at the steaming flesh. He ate like a starving wolf. The tender white meat had a sweet flavor, a delicacy he had never enjoyed in New Archangel.

Chapter 15

The next morning Alexi set out to explore to the north. He paddled between small islands and the shore most of the morning, and at mid-day reached a large bay. The waters in the middle of the bay were churned by a strong wind blowing down from the mountains. He paddled into the bay, following the shoreline and discovered a banquet.

A small stream spilled over a jumbled bed of rocks. Masses of wriggling salmon, their bodies mottled brown and red, choked the entrance to the stream. Alexi stopped a dozen paces from the stream and pulled his baidarka beyond the reach of the tide. He took his spear and approached the stream cautiously, scanning the shoreline for bears. The salmon scattered as he neared the edge of the stream, but settled into the current when he stood still. He continued to stalk the salmon, pausing after each step to let the fish settle down.

Soon he had one foot in the frigid water, his spear poised to strike. He waited patiently, studying the fish as they moved in the stream. The fish had moved to the other bank, beyond his reach. He waded deeper into the stream, closer to the fish, only to have them change directions and flow in behind him.

Try as he might, he was unable to spear even one fish. He sank to the ground on the bank, soaked from his shirttail to his boots. Elation had become frustration. He sat with his head between his knees and thought. As he sat, he hatched a plan.

Alexi studied the river. There were several deep pools in which the salmon gathered. Each of the fish awaited some mysterious signal that would send them shooting through the shallows that separated the pools. His idea came from the Kolosh boys he had seen fishing in a river near the fort.

He retrieved his axe and cut an armful of sturdy alder poles two fingers in diameter. He carried the poles to the rapids above the first pool. He drove the sharpened sticks into the bed of the stream, building a fence that angled from the center of the rapids to the shore. The fence narrowed to a chute as it approached the shore.

Alexi waded to the far bank and waited for the fish in the pool below the fence to settle, then he charged into the stream. He carried a short stick in each hand and beat the water as he moved toward the fence.

The fish scattered in all directions, but a few swam between the fence and shore. He ran forward, herding the panicked fish into his trap. Three plump salmon were wedged against the shore. Alexi dropped his sticks and charged the final paces, using his hands to heave the fish onto the bank. The salmon flopped on the shore, trying to find their way back to the water. He tossed each further from the water's edge until he was sure they wouldn't escape.

He raised his hands over his head in celebration and danced around his catch. When he turned toward the stream his breath froze in his throat. Standing ten paces away was a massive brown bear. The bruin stood broadside, his huge belly nearly reaching the ground. The hair on the top of the bear's shoulder hump stood at attention and he stared at Alexi with beady black eyes.

The fish now belonged to him. Alexi backed slowly down

the beach, keeping his eyes on the bear. The bear sauntered over to the nearest fish and gently bit down on the middle of the salmon. The bear kept a single eye on Alexi as he pinned the fish to the ground with a long, sharp claw and ripped open the fish's belly. The bear licked the red eggs from the female salmon and took a few bites of flesh then moved on to the second fish.

Alexi remained a statue. In all of the adventures around the fort, he had never encountered a bear at such close quarters. The men in New Archangel had the highest respect for the king of the forest, and made every effort to steer clear of them. Alexi had done the same, and was unprepared for this encounter. His instincts told him to run for his boat, but he had a sense that the bear was not after him. It would eat his fish and offer no thanks.

Alexi inched backward without taking his eyes off of the bear. The bear paid little attention to the unwelcome guest and moved to the third salmon.

When Alexi could see his baidarka out of the corner of his eye, he turned and walked to the boat. His axe was still lying in the pile of trimmings at the edge of the alder thicket. He launched his boat and glided away from the shore. Once in deep water, he turned the boat to face the bear.

The thief had finished his ill-gotten gain and now fished for himself in the shallows. Alexi watched as the bear caught and devoured several more fish. The bear's speed and fishing skills were impressive. Alexi was glad that he hadn't made the attempt to run. The bear would have had little difficulty chasing him down even with a generous head start. The sky had begun to darken, and he decided to leave the bear. He would return for the axe and would be better prepared to face the bear.

Dinner was soup of carrots, turnips and pork. A dinner of

fresh salmon would have to wait.

As he ate his soup, Alexi looked over the long guns. Both of the weapons had begun to rust in spots as he had no oil to spread on them.

He opened the keg of powder and emptied a handful of powder into the powder horn. The black mixture sparkled in the light of the fire and he breathed in the aroma of sulfur. He sewed a small pouch from a scrap of sail cloth and a wooden needle whittled from an alder twig. He filled the pouch with a dozen lead balls.

As the fire died out, Alexi pointed a long gun into the night, practicing holding the heavy weapon steady on targets at various distances. He tucked a long gun, the powder horn, and pouch of shot beside him when he crawled under his furs. Sleep came easily, and he dreamed of his father's stew and the pool of warm light from an oil lamp.

Dawn broke under low clouds. Alexi rose and stirred his fire to life. He had begun to bank his fire before he slept so he could quickly regenerate the flames. He reheated the soup and finished it. Tonight he would dine on salmon.

Alexi loaded a long gun and shot pouch into the baidarka, and pushed off in the direction of the stream. The seas were more restless and he wondered if there was another storm approaching. He paddled along the shore, rising and falling to the rhythm of the swells.

The bay was calm. Alexi paddled to the same place he had landed the day before. The fish were thick, waiting to climb the rapids. He scanned the shoreline in both directions for signs of the bear, and he looked long and hard into the thicket. Seeing nothing, he beached his boat and headed for his trap.

The line of poles stood tall. A large school of fish was milling around near the mouth of the trap.

Alexi sat down and removed the ram rod from the stock of the long gun. He poured a small amount of black powder from the powder horn down the muzzle. He then placed a small cloth patch over the barrel and put a ball in the center of the patch. The ball and patch went down smoothly under the ramrod, firmly seating against the powder. He poured a small amount of powder on the flash pan and gently closed the lock to seal the powder.

Flintlocks were sensitive tools and the powder stored in the pan would not ignite when wet so care had to be taken to keep it dry. He laid the loaded weapon on the shore near the mouth of the trap.

Wading knee-deep in the river, he charged the mouth of the trap. As he pounded the surface of the water, the fish scattered, some choosing his narrowing channel. He drove the salmon into his trap, catching half a dozen. Two escaped while he attempted to toss them onto the shore.

He looked in all directions for the bear. He was alone. Using a stone, he stunned each fish with a blow to the head. He carried the fish to his baidarka on a run and returned as quickly for his long gun. He remembered the axe and retrieved it from the pile of branches where he had left it the day before. He slipped his boat into the water, pushing the fish behind him and the long gun forward beneath the bow. He would dine well tonight.

Having made his escape with no sign of the bear, he felt inclined to do some exploring. He turned the boat east and worked his way deeper into the bay. The beach stretched far into the distance before turning south and disappearing. The far shore was over two leagues distant. Shortly after leaving the stream, he came upon a clearing with the skeletons of several structures fashioned from small trees.

It was a Kolosh camp. Alexi nosed the baidarka onto the

shore. He carried his long gun to the clearing to look around. There were fresh bear tracks in soft mud. The frame in the center of the clearing was ready for some kind of covering. The soil under the structure was worn smooth.

Footpaths led to two other frameworks and joined to form a wider trail to the shoreline. There was a mound of soggy black ash near the shoreline and scattered about the fire pit were the bones of large animals. There was no moss on the bones and the ground around the fire pit was free of the shoots of grass.

Alexi breathed a sigh of relief. The Kolosh had already come and gone. If the camp had been unused, the trails and floors would be overgrown. The only items of interest were two large racks near the trees on the north side of the clearing. He walked around the wooden rails, realizing what they were for once the wind brought the smell to his nose. The racks had been used to smoke and dry fish. The wood smelled strongly of smoke and fish oil. He decided to smoke some fish for himself.

Chapter 16

Back at camp, Alexi split three of the fish down each side of the backbone, stopping a few fingers from the tail. He removed the backbone and head from the carcass, leaving the two strips of bright red meat attached to the tail. He would hang them over his fire to smoke. He removed the head and guts from the fourth fish, and then cut the fish into steaks. He left the other half of the fish for tomorrow's meal. Tonight he would feast.

Smoking fish required salt. He walked to the shore and scooped a pot of water. He carried the pot back to the fire and set it on the coals. Soon steam began to rise in great puffs. Alexi left the water to boil and went to the trees behind his camp and cut down a bundle of fur.

The hides were crusted white with salt. Alexi cleaned the furs while he waited for the water to boil away. When he had finished the first bundle of fur, he returned to the fire. A thin layer of salt covered the bottom and sides of the empty pot. Alexi lifted the pot from the coals with a hooked stick and set it on the moss. Steam shot from under the pot as it settled into the damp moss. When the pot was cool Alexi used his knife to scrape the salt crystals into his second pot.

He cleaned fur and dried salt until it was time for dinner. Dinner was fried salmon sprinkled with salt. Oil bubbled from the flesh as it cooked, making his mouth water in anticipation. He diced a carrot into the pan, turning the orange pieces in the oily fish drippings. While his meal cooked, he fetched a large mug of fresh water. The smell of the fish became irresistible and he removed the pot from the fire and tore off a piece of the succulent flesh. The steaming meat melted in his mouth. Tears welled in his eyes as the hot fish burned him, but still he chewed. He quenched his tongue with cold water and devoured two of the salmon steaks and the carrots. He had never eaten so well.

It was far into the night before the furs were all clean and hung again in the tree. His pot was overflowing with salt.

Darkness had seeped into the forest and Alexi could see a few stars peeking from behind the fading blanket of clouds as he fell asleep.

The next morning, sunlight filtered through the trees and shone brightly in his eyes. A light frost covered the ground. Alexi huddled in his bedroll, reluctant to leave the warmth of the fur.

He ate the remaining salmon for breakfast and then spent an hour cutting poles from the alder thicket, lashing them with lengths of line to form a rack over his fire pit.

Alexi hung the salmon fillets on the rack. He cut slices every two or three fingers down their length and spread a layer of salt over the surface of the meat. When the fish was ready he coaxed a fire from the coals and fed it small pieces of alder. The alder burned slowly and produced a heavy smoke. The smoke hovered above the fire and spread over the salmon. Alexi left the fish to smoke and hiked across the island.

On the island's outer shoreline, piles of drifted wood lay jumbled on the rocky shoreline. Alexi picked through the piles, selecting four pieces of wood. Using a length of line he lashed two pieces of wood together in the shape of a cross and wedged its base into the rocks at the shoreline. The cross stood taller than his head and would serve as a marker to approaching boats.

He carried the remaining pieces of wood back to camp. While he watched the smoke rise over the fish, he fashioned a grave marker for his friend.

He added more alder to the fire and then carried the marker to the cook's grave and buried the base deep in the pile of rocks. He would return one day to pay his respects to his friend and place a proper marker.

The sun quickly drove away the morning chill, and by the time it reached its peak Alexi had added to his supply of firewood and the fish were smoking nicely. As the tide receded, he searched the beach for what food there might be at his doorstep.

He found the oval shaped, leathery creatures that he had seen the Kolosh prying from the rocks the day before he had left New Archangel. Red and purple urchins gathered among the stones just beneath the water. They could be eaten in an emergency, but with salmon abundant a short distance from his camp he left them where they were.

His vegetables would soon be gone, and he would need a supply of greens. He picked among the seaweeds until he found a type that had small wrinkled leaves and was dark green. He had watched the Kolosh gather this type of seaweed. He gathered several handfuls and headed back up the shore. The sun lit the trees a brilliant green and blue smoke drifted up through their branches carrying the aroma of the smoking fish.

He spread the seaweed over rocks at the edge of the alders. It would dry quickly and he could store it for use when his carrots and turnips were gone.

The fire smoldered, producing delicious smoke. The red flesh was coated with a smooth and shiny skin that would seal the moisture in the meat. The fillets had stiffened and would dry further in storage. Such a fine delicacy would likely attract passing animals, so he decided he would cache his stores high in the trees.

Alexi spent the remainder of the morning sewing cloth bags and filling them with potatoes, turnips and carrots. He hung the bags from the branches of the thickest spruce. He cut away the lower branches, leaving enough of each branch sticking out to make a ladder to reach the bags. He left one bag empty on the ground in which to store the smoked fish.

He returned to the fire and collected the fish. The stiff fillets smelled delightful and he broke off a piece and ate it. The flavor was perfect and he devoured half of one fish before he could stop.

Alexi put the remaining smoked fish into the cloth bag and hung it with the others. He spent the rest of the day tidying up his camp and inspecting the long guns. He examined the firing mechanisms and his shooting supplies, planning how he would carry them. He practiced loading the weapons in his baidarka.

The next morning Alexi went exploring to the south of his island. A gentle swell rolled in from the northwest and the sea was smooth. He poked in and out of the rocks and small islands. He watched small fish in the shallows darting about and saw several crabs that were too deep in the water to spear.

Alexi headed out to sea. When the sun had reached its peak he was several leagues from shore. He spent the afternoon drifting and studying the snow covered peaks and the shoreline that stretched far to the southwest. It would be a difficult paddle to New Archangel, but if a rescue party did not return within three or four weeks' time, he would be forced to make the journey. He wasn't sure he could survive winter. The storms that rolled into the sound forced the people of New Archangel into their cabins for weeks on end. His thin canvas and bundle of furs would be no match for the fierce weather.

As the sun moved toward the horizon, Alexi lined up the blaze with the peak of the mountain and headed toward his island. As he neared the shoreline, a head popped up, facing away from Alexi. The seal had not noticed his approach and Alexi drifted not twenty paces from the animal.

The seal would provide meat and a warm hide. His heart raced as he slid the long gun from between his legs. With great care, he laid the heavy weapon across the cockpit in front of him and dug out a small pinch of powder from the horn around his neck. As he sprinkled the powder on the flash pan, the seal drifted on the surface unaware of his baidarka.

The spotted animal tilted its nose toward the sky and slipped under the surface. Alexi pulled back the hammer on the flintlock and closed the frizzen to seal the powder in the pan. He sat absolutely still and waited.

A few moments later the seal returned to the surface. Alexi had drifted even closer and the spots on the seal's short coat were clearly visible. He raised the long gun and trained it on the unsuspecting animal. The bobbing of the boat made keeping the sights on the seal's small head difficult, but he waited and concentrated. Satisfied with his aim, Alexi squeezed the trigger. A cloud of smoke and fire erupted from the barrel of the gun.

The seal arched skyward at the shock of the explosion, but was dead before it knew it had been struck. He nearly dropped the long gun into the water as he scrambled to put it below decks. His hands were shaking. The seal bobbed on its side. A red cloud trailed off in the current. He maneuvered beside the dead seal and slipped a lanyard around its flipper. With the seal secured to the baidarka, he paddled toward shore. Excitement kept him paddling without tiring.

As he passed between the cliffs, Alexi wondered what to do with the seal, now that he had killed it. The hide and meat would be useful, but how to prepare the animal was a matter he hadn't considered in the excitement of the hunt. The daylight was fading fast and he would deal with the seal in the morning. He tied a line to the seal and secured it to a tree as darkness fell.

The coals were still glowing and Alexi nursed them to life. He dined on boiled turnips and carrots. With the fire burning brightly, he poured hot water down the barrel of the long gun and pulled a patch of cloth up and down the barrel to rinse out the residue left from his shot on the seal. With the gun as clean as he could make it in the darkness, he made up his bed against the cold that accompanied the darkness.

The waves thundered against invisible rocks. The icy water stung his flesh. He clung to the broken piece of wood with all of his strength, but the crashing waves tried to rip loose his grip and separate him from the only thing in the sea that could save his life. Suddenly a huge wave tore the piece of wood from his hands. He was plunged deep under the surface. The air in his lungs burned to be free. He held his breath and struggled to find the surface. Something bumped hard against his back, he spun to find out what it was and the white and bloated face of the cook stared back with empty gaping eyes. He screamed...

His scream woke Alexi from his nightmare. The forest was black, his fire nothing more than a glow. He was sweating. He opened his covers and let the cold air flood over his body.

Chapter 17

When daylight came, Alexi rose and ate an apple. He decided to eat one for breakfast each day until they were gone. He counted them. Fifteen remained. He made a second decision as well. If the apples were gone and no one had returned for the fur, he would set out for New Archangel on his own. That settled, he put the lid back on the small crate and returned it to his storehouse.

The seal floated near the shore, just as it had the night before. He pulled the animal from the water and dragged it up the beach. The silver fur was dappled with black spots. The large brown eyes were open but glazed over with a cloudy film.

He was happy he had killed an animal and would make good use of it. At the same time he was saddened that an animal as beautiful as this had to die. He thought of the fur seals, sea otter and other creatures that the Russian hunters slaughtered with the help of the Aleut hunters. He thought of the bundles of fur hanging like ghosts in the trees behind his camp.

He began skinning the seal. He had watched the men skinning otter and seal many times on the docks in the harbor. But now, as he looked at the seal, he wished he had paid more attention.

He cut around the seal's flippers, opening the skin to the flesh and spilling rivulets of blood over the fur. He slit the fur along the seal's belly to just below its throat. With care he began to skin the hide away from the thick layer of fat. It was slow going, but he gained confidence with each stroke of his knife and was soon working his way around the seal's back.

It took the better part of the morning to remove the seal's skin, but he had done a neat job of it. The soft white fat was crisscrossed by trails of blood. Alexi shaved the fat from the animal's body and piled it on a square of canvas.

With the fat removed, the bluish flesh of the muscular animal lay exposed. Seal intestines were a fine waterproof material so he opened the seal's stomach, spilling its entrails down the beach. The smell was pungent and he staggered back.

After letting the air clear, Alexi cut away a long strip of intestine and squeezed its contents into the sea, coiling the tube on the tarp beside the pile of fat. He cut away at the exposed flesh and soon a pile of meat larger than the fat was stacked on the canvas.

The bones and head of the seal stared blankly at him. He dragged the remains to the top of the cliff that overlooked the entrance to the lagoon and pushed it over the cliff. He watched as it disappeared into the dark water.

Alexi returned to camp and collected the empty potato barrel and his pots. He set them beside the pile of flesh. He gathered some firewood and soon had a fire burning on the beach. Broken clouds occasionally let the sun shine through.

Once the fire was burning strong, he filled the pots to overflowing with the slippery fat and set them at the edge of the fire. He loaded handfuls of the dark meat into the barrel and rolled it back to his camp. At camp he transferred the meat to a canvas tarp.

He returned to the beach with the empty barrel and stood it by the fire. The white fat began to settle and melt into a yellow liquid. When the pile of fat had melted, Alexi poured the oil into the barrel. The seams on the wooden container remained snugly sealed and only a tiny amount of oil leaked from between the staves.

He divided his time between smoking seal meat and melting the remaining fat. He cut several long sections from the intestines and spread them in a shallow pool near the water to soak clean. At day's end, he had filled a canvas bag with the blackened meat and had a third of a keg of oil.

The first use he made of the oil was to rub a coating over the rusting long guns. The red spots of rust vanished beneath the aromatic oil. The seal oil had a powerful odor but Alexi had grown used to it.

For dinner he boiled a potato and a turnip and sliced thin pieces of smoked seal meat. The meat was chewy and had a strong flavor, but was rich and oily and a small amount satisfied his hunger. With darkness approaching he decided to try something he had pondered since killing the seal.

He searched the shoreline and found a large clamshell. He cut a short length of twine and laid it in the clamshell. Using another shell as a ladle he dipped a portion of the seal's oil and poured it over the twine and filled the shell to the top with the thick oil.

Alexi stuck the end of a small stick into the glowing embers. In a moment the stick caught fire. He removed the flaming tip from the fire and touched it to the end of the oil-soaked twine. A feeble flicker of yellow hung over the small cord for a moment, reluctantly growing to a steady flame as the oil caught fire and burned on the heavy fibers. The light from his lamp flickered on his face. He longed for a book to read. He let the lamp burn beside him at the edge of the fire, celebrating the small achievement. Alexi planned the next few days as he basked in the warmth of the fire.

The sun shone brightly the next morning, but the days were getting shorter. Soon enough, the darkness would win the battle for the sky and the country would be plunged into long winter nights. After gathering his tools and downing an apple, Alexi set out for the stream. The water was calm and the still air had a crispness that confirmed a change in the season. The leaves on some of the willows along the shore had exchanged their summer green for yellow.

At the stream there were fewer fish than before. Alexi looked for any sign of the bear, but saw none. His fish trap was intact, and he was able to beach a dozen salmon. Soaking wet and cold, he returned to camp with his baidarka heavily loaded.

The next two days were spent smoking salmon and working on the seal skin. Alexi had watched the hunters in New Archangel work seal hides and he began to do as he had seen. He bent a sturdy spruce bough into a hoop, and lashed it with rope. He stretched the hide inside of the hoop and tied it in place with strips of gut. He scraped the remaining fat from the flesh, taking care not to cut through the hide.

When the hide was cleaned, he spread a layer of salt over the skin to cure it. The lengths of intestine he had saved from the seal's gut made an excellent liner for his shot and powder pouches. He stitched small pouches using strips of intestine for thread.

After two days, Alexi had a large bundle of fish hanging in a cloth bag in the tree and waterproof pouches for his shot and powder. The wind changed on the second afternoon, and blew from the northwest. The temperature dropped. He paddled south for several hours landing in a narrow cove. The beach was a jumble of large rounded stones.

Alexi set up a bear cracker, a growth the size of a skillet plucked from a spruce tree. The underside of the bear cracker was bright white and easily seen from fifty paces. He used it as a target to hone his shooting skills.

After a dozen slow reloads Alexi was able to put the ball near the center of his target. Satisfied with his progress, and irritated by the loud report of the long gun echoing over the silence, Alexi headed back to his camp.

He dined on smoked fish and potatoes. He boiled some water and poured it down the barrel of the long gun. He worked a patch of cloth soaked in seal oil up and down the inside of the barrel to clean it. His chores finished, he carved a fourteenth notch in the root. There had been no sign of a ship.

Three bears had been fishing at the stream on his last visit and while he had enjoyed watching them, he was unable to catch any more fish. Fewer fish in the stream confirmed that the season was slipping away. Flocks of geese and cranes had been passing overhead, their raucous calls echoing over the empty shoreline. He decided it was time to return to New Archangel.

Two storms swept over his island in the days that followed, allowing only brief forays beyond the lagoon. Alexi planned his voyage to New Archangel during the long hours spent watching the rain fall in sheets.

Departure

Chapter 18

On his twentieth morning on the island Alexi was up and moving as the sunlight began creeping into the forest. He had spent a week preparing to leave the island. The furs were secure in the upper boughs of the tall spruce, wrapped in sailcloth to keep out vermin and pitch. His baidarka had been freshly coated with seal oil to protect the hide against the icy water that would test the boat for long hours each day.

His stores of powder and shot were tucked neatly under the deck of his baidarka. The furs he used for his bed were stowed forward in the narrow bow.

Wrapped in the furs was his supply of dried fish. He estimated his supplies would last twenty days. He would eat berries from the forest and seaweed, crab and clams from the shore as he traveled.

The long guns, the axe, the best pot, his clothes and a square of sailcloth that would serve as his shelter were packed into the stern of the boat. The pot was filled with the remaining potatoes. There was barely room in the cramped baidarka for his legs.

He opened the crate and picked up the last apple. It was mushy but still very sweet. He took small bites, savoring each as he ground it between his teeth. His fire pit was cold.

A large mound of ashes was all that remained from the many nights he had huddled close for warmth. When he finished his apple, he walked down his well-worn trail to the cook's grave.

His friend would be alone. He adjusted the marker, adding a few extra rocks to strengthen it.

"Good bye, my friend. I will remember you to your family, that I promise you," Alexi's spoken words sounded strange. He had spoken aloud only a few times since he had landed on the island. He said a short prayer for his friend, silently this time, then strode back to his baidarka.

He had timed his departure for high tide. The boat settled low in the water as Alexi slipped in, wriggling his feet into the empty spaces.

The boat rode steady, much lower in the water than normal, but with ample freeboard. He pushed away from the shore and dipped his paddle. The boat moved slowly at first, resisting the extra load. But soon he was making good time. The sleek craft cut a smooth line through green water.

Scores of jellyfish undulated beneath him, red and white with crosses on their domed backs. Clusters of long flowing tentacles stretched out beneath them.

The clouds hung on the horizon hiding the mountains. He was glad he couldn't see the mountains, for their white blanket had crept down, forewarning the coming of winter. His spirits were high. Soon, he told himself, he would be walking the muddy streets of New Archangel. His father would be proud of him. He knew his father would never give up on him.

He paddled south between the rocks and islands. The ocean was calm and the gentle swells rolled in, lifting him in a rocking motion.

He stopped in the early afternoon and stretched his legs

in the forest and snacked on blueberries. He shared the berry patch with a pair of purple jays, who protested his intrusion.

By late afternoon, his arms were numb and his shoulders felt as though they were on fire. He entered a small cove between jagged cliffs and beached his baidarka. He chose a spot under the high branches of a large spruce and turned his flint to the steel on a pile of tinder. While the fire grew, he spread his canvas and gathered an armload of hemlock branches for his bed.

A dinner of dried salmon and a handful of berries satisfied his hunger. As darkness fell, a few stars appeared between the lumpy clouds.

There was a light frost on the ground when Alexi crawled from under his bedroll. He stirred his fire to life and warmed his hands and feet. The sun hadn't peeked over the mountains, but the day was beginning to brighten. He finished the berries he had gathered the night before and another strip of salmon and made his way to the shore. A trickle of water ran down the face of a cliff. He took a long drink. His muscles were stiff but he welcomed the discomfort. It meant he was closer to New Archangel.

After re-packing the baidarka, he pressed on. The shoreline became more rugged at midday, and Alexi had to venture onto the open sea.

A slight breeze came at the boat bow-on. The sharp nose of the baidarka sliced through the small waves as it rose and fell with the swells. He slipped easily over the ocean, and soon the barrier islands and reefs reappeared. Alexi slipped behind a treeless island and studied the shoreline.

A small stream tumbled down a rock face beyond a peninsula, emptying into a small pool. He could make out the ripples created by schooling salmon. He drifted motionless a few boat lengths away from shore.

The stream ran only a few dozen paces before climbing to the waterfall. Alexi paddled beyond the stream and beached his boat. He slipped into the forest and cut a stout alder spear and sharpened the end.

Returning to the shore, he edged close to the pool. The salmon didn't scatter. He guessed no bears fished on the stream. Alexi crouched and moved with the spear cocked behind his right ear. When he peered over the edge of the pool, he paused and sized up the salmon. These fish were smaller and were marked with a brown band over their white bellies. Many had humps behind their heads with hooked noses and sharp teeth.

He studied the fish as they circled the pool and taking aim drove his spear into the water and held it pinned to the bottom. The fish exploded in a frenzy. When the water settled, a fish wriggled on the end of his spear. Alexi dragged the twisting, speared fish across the bottom and it onto the shore.

Dropping the spear, he carried the salmon away from the pool and stunned it with a stone. Alexi gutted the fish and dropped it on the rocky shore. He built a fire and soon had a bed of glowing coals. He split the fish down the back and sprinkled a bit of salt over the pink flesh before laying it in the coals.

He made camp between two large trees and lashed his baidarka to a tree.

With his camp set, he pulled the steaming fish from the coals and picked the flesh from the bones, working his way from the head to the tail. Alexi saved a piece of fish for breakfast and then slipped into the forest for a dessert of berries.

He slept soundly, without dreaming.

Chapter 19

The weather continued cloudy and mild for two days and Alexi made good progress toward home. He dined on crab and slices of the kelp stalk that grew on the rocks. Each evening he made a camp at the edge of the forest, rising early to make his way toward home and his father. By his estimate, he might be half way back to New Archangel.

On the evening of the fifth day the sky cleared to blue. Alexi could see the sharp peak of the great mountain, it was more distant than he expected. His heart soared at his progress. He slept well under his furs.

After washing his cold breakfast down with a long drink from a stream, Alexi paddled on the open sea most of the day. The sky was a deep blue and a westerly breeze rocked the boat as it glided over gentle swells.

In the distance, the shore was hidden by a peninsula that stretched far to sea. It took most of the morning to reach the peninsula. As he rounded the point, his heart fell. He faced a vast sound. He could just make out the fuzzy shapes of tiny trees on the opposite shore. He was suddenly tired. To the south there were no snow-covered mountains. The snow-capped cone of the volcano, which served as sentinel to New Archangel was not visible. The crossing would be lengthy and would require good weather. The wind had come up again, and the sound was very choppy.

He decided to make camp. He would cross the sound the

next day with his body and mind well-rested if the weather permitted. He paddled into an inlet carved between steep stone walls. The shore in the cove was gradual and inviting. He pulled his baidarka up and made his camp. He slept in the shadow of a hemlock tree and dreamed of the muddy paths in the fort, and of the Kolosh children on the beach gathering sea creatures.

Morning brought a deep blue sky, backlit by the rising sun. The ocean was as smooth as glass. Alexi ate breakfast and stared across the sound. He wondered how far he would travel to reach New Archangel.

As he packed his boat, he checked his stores. He had plenty of smoked fish, and the berries were thick in the forest. He tucked his long guns into the boat and slipped into his intestine coat. He lashed the compass to the top of his baidarka just in front of the cockpit. His boat would be sealed against the waves and retrieving the compass from his pocket would not be possible. He fastened the hem of his coat around the cockpit with a lanyard to keep out water if the seas got rough.

Soon after pushing off, Alexi slipped beyond the last rocky outcropping and entered the sound. A group of large islands were scattered deep into the sound to the east and heavy clouds hovered over their tops.

The tide was at its lowest as Alexi set out. The rising sun was a sparkling yellow streak across the water. He paddled steadily, distancing himself from the shore.

As he moved further from shore, a gentle breeze began to blow out of the sound. The wind chilled his sweating face and neck. He shivered. His bow was pointed south by southwest, but his eyes told him he was moving in a different direction. Lining up marks on the far shore Alexi realized that the tide was pushing him into the sound. He corrected his course seaward of the furthest point of land.

As he approached the middle of the sound a thin mist formed over the water, and quickly grew thicker. Alexi took a bearing on the shore.

Alexi was soon engulfed in a blinding white cloud. The fog nearly hid the bow of his baidarka. He paddled with his eyes focused on the compass, trying to keep his course steady. The water was becoming choppy.

Suddenly, the surface of the water began to dance. At first tiny ripples moved in all directions at once and then the waves were breaking over the bow and stern. The water became violent very quickly, and Alexi abandoned his course to keep the boat from swamping. Waves swarmed from all sides at once and the baidarka bobbed and shook violently as wave after wave passed over and under the craft. He was soaked by the spray blown from the tops of the waves. He shook the water from his face and wiped his eyes on the sleeve of his coat.

Large rafts of kelp swirled beside him, diving below the surface as if pulled under by hidden hands. Alexi's shoulders burned, and his stomach cramped. Waves higher than his head tossed the boat like a soggy cork. He glanced down to check his course and panic swept over him. A wave had stolen the compass from under his nose.

Alexi paddled blindly, fighting to keep the boat upright. The wind increased and the waves became more unpredictable. The fire that burned in his shoulders crept down his arms and back. He paused to catch his breath. As he rested the paddle across the deck, a low and steady sucking sound began to grow behind him. He turned his head to look and his eyes flew wide in fright.

A huge whirlpool spun into a swirling pit. The water around the whirlpool was smooth and Alexi and his boat were in the path of the monster. He dug his paddle deeply, pulling with every ounce of his strength, fearing that it might snap. The water around him grew calm as the churning waves were pushed aside by the whirlpool.

The bow dipped over the lip of the whirlpool and the baidarka plunged toward the center. The churning water turned him in a circle. Alexi paddled furiously and the boat leapt ahead, making another revolution before shooting out the whirlpool and back into the waves.

Relief flooded through him, but his good fortune was brief as the angry sea again slammed his boat. Water ran down his face and dripped from his matted hair. The fog was so thick that he could barely make out the next wave.

The weight of his supplies was quickly draining his energy. He struggled to keep paddling as his arms began to refuse his commands. Suddenly a huge wave rose up beneath him, lifting his boat on a cushion of green, frothy water. The boat hesitated for a moment then slid down the face of the wave, plunging bow first beneath the surface. He held his breath and pulled his paddle close to the side of the baidarka and waited.

Slowly, very slowly, the boat rose to the surface, upside down. Alexi pulled his paddle against his body, extending the blade deep into the water, until it hung below his head. He swung the blade in a powerful arc, leaning back against the deck as he pulled on the paddle. The baidarka rolled on the surface and Alexi emerged from the water. The cockpit once again faced the sky and he rejoined the battle against the sea.

The sucking sound came again, this time from several directions at once, and Alexi could make out rafts of seaweed, swirling madly in the current. The water was trying to drag his boat under. Alexi fought on. The water moved in great swirling boils. The fog was a heavy wet blanket, blocking his sight.

As quickly as they had appeared, the churning waves subsided and he drifted over tall, undulating swells. The sudden silence was eerie. The soggy boat raced along on fast moving water. Alexi used his paddle sparingly and rested. He was utterly lost. The tide had been rising when he left the cape. He guessed he might be near the islands and he kept an ear cocked, listening for birds or surf. He heard only the gentle sloshing of the water.

His aching shoulders had come close to giving out and he worked them gently to relieve the pain. Tiny whirlpools, dwarves compared to the monster he had encountered earlier, appeared and disappeared around the boat, sucking in air as they collapsed. Alexi longed for the compass which now rested on the bottom.

The sun was little more than a soft glow above the dense fog. As time passed Alexi dozed, unable to fight off his need for rest. He slumped forward, his forearms resting on his paddle.

Chapter 20

A gentle bumping sound woke Alexi from his slumber. He looked up, raising his head slowly. The water had turned dirty brown and the fog had vanished. It had been replaced by a mass of brilliant white, rhythmically bumping against the side of the baidarka. Alexi sat tall and stared at a mountain of ice. It dwarfed his boat. In every direction huge pieces of ice littered the smooth surface of the sea. Where was he? Was this still part of a dream?

Stretching out his hand, he ran his fingers over the frozen surface. He recoiled. What was this place? Tree-covered mountains ringed the field of floating ice. The ice stretched away in all directions. Though a mass of thick clouds overhead obscured the sun, he could make out a spot of brightness to his starboard.

A tall headland to the south rose sharply from the water. A grassy area at the top of the low mountain would afford a vantage point from which he could gain his bearings. He dipped his paddle and set out for the shore.

The icebergs were scattered and he easily made his way between them. Some were massive, towering high above his head, while others weren't much larger than his boat.

Small fish schooled at the surface. Hungry gulls plunged into the water and surfaced with fish in their beaks. High overhead, eagles circled in graceful arcs, searching with their sharp eyes for an easy meal. Near the shoreline, the current shifted and the water was clearer and free of ice.

The shoreline was rocky and strewn with the remains of trees and branches cast on the beach by recent storms. Like silver hatpins, the trees were scattered in clusters against the alder thicket. The bow scraped shore and he crawled stiffly from his boat. He lashed the baidarka to a sturdy alder and sat on a flat stone to rest. He rubbed his aching legs, urging the blood to return and scanned the water. Ice was scattered in all directions. Everything looked the same. He stretched for a moment then set about making camp. He needed rest before he climbed the mountain.

As night fell, Alexi sat by the fire, chewing smoked salmon and blueberries. When he began to doze, he lay down in his bedroll with his long gun beside him and fell asleep.

Morning brought steady rains and gusty winds. He took out a long gun, shot and powder and tucked his fire tools in his pocket. Alexi started up the hill behind his camp. Thick brush made the climbing difficult.

Mixed among the berry bushes, were huge patches of devil's club. The nasty, broad-leafed plants carpeted the forest floor. The undersides of their leaves were covered with rows of thorns. The stalk of the plant, the size of a man's thumb, was completely covered with lethal spikes. The wiry, vicious plants slowed him further. Devil's club offered no safe hand holds for climbing.

He skirted a large patch of the spiny plants and found a deer trail that led up the hill. After an hour's time, he broke free of the underbrush, emerging onto a gradual slope carpeted with lilies and dotted with scrub spruce. Small, shallow ponds were scattered amongst the lilies, their bottoms covered in soft mud. The muddy bottoms were a trick. Men had sunk over their heads in the muck.

As he reached the top of the hill, the sea below became

visible. He could see patches of dark water scattered with icebergs. The strait below him had arms that stretched in all directions. In the distance he could see a massive wall of ice, the source of the icebergs. With the sun blocked by heavy clouds and without the compass he could not be certain which channel led back to the sound.

He despaired at the confusing expanse of water and ice below him. The breeze swept over the ridge, chilling him. He wrapped his coat tightly around his shoulders and crawled under a stand of spruce.

Alexi thought. He had ample provisions for two more weeks, and could likely secure fresh fish in a nearby stream. The berries were heavy on the bushes and would last into early winter. He wouldn't starve but he was lost. He had heard of an inland route from New Archangel to grounds where the Company traded with the inland tribes and the Kolosh, but he had no map. He might find his way to New Archangel if he had some idea of how to navigate the confusing channels. He lay back and closed his eyes.

Alexi dozed into the afternoon. As light began to fade, the clouds descended. The rain became a damp mist. He was no closer to a plan than he had been when he had started up the hill. He was tired, even though he had slept, and the chill had slipped beneath his coat. He gathered his long gun and made his way down to the beach. The clouds followed him down the mountain.

The baidarka bobbed gently at the water's edge. Evening was approaching, and he decided that tomorrow he would work his way along the shoreline to find another hill from which to survey when the weather improved. Perhaps he would find a passage that would take him back to the coast.

Alexi lay under his tarp, listening to the steady thump of raindrops and the chatter of birds as they settled down for the night. In the distance he could hear a whale blowing. Sleep finally came as his small fire faded to dim, red coals.

He broke camp the next morning under a downpour. His intestine coat kept him dry as he paddled. The shoreline was broken by occasional bluffs topped by tall spruce. The heavy rain hid the mountains. He grew discouraged by the foul weather and decided to make camp on the next point and wait for the weather to clear. He would eat berries and look for a salmon stream.

As he drifted near the shoreline, something caught his eye. A few hundred paces ahead there appeared to be a log with something snagged on the end. It wasn't a bird, for it was low to the water and more rounded. He was convinced that he had seen movement. Curiosity drew him to investigate as the mist played tricks on his eyes.

As he drew near, he saw it wasn't a log. A long ridge ran the length of the object, plunging at both ends in well-formed curves. The log became an overturned canoe. Someone clung to one end.

Alexi's skin covered in goose bumps and he scanned in all directions for signs of other canoes. It was a Kolosh canoe. He was in their territory. His instincts told him to turn and paddle for all he was worth but he knew that the person clinging to the canoe was also clinging to life.

With a final glance toward the point behind him, Alexi paddled to the canoe. When he came alongside, he saw a boy about his own age.

The Kolosh had thick black hair, which was matted over his brown face. He had one arm over the canoe and held the sharp keel wedged in his armpit. With his other hand, he clung to the bow stem. His eyes were closed and he appeared lifeless. Alexi called out and the Kolosh lifted leaden eyelids. His eyes were dull. His energy was almost gone.

Alexi maneuvered alongside the boy. He untied the skirt of his jacket and slipped the line under the arm draped over the canoe. He worked the lanyard over the Kolosh's head and shoulders and pulled the loop tight.

He spoke loudly and the Kolosh boy opened his eyes a slit.

"Let go and grab my boat," He gestured as he yelled, urging the Kolosh to take hold of the baidarka. The Kolosh seemed to understand, even in his stupor, and he slid from the canoe. He immediately sank beneath the surface and pulled heavily against the lanyard. The weight of the boy tipped the baidarka to a dangerous angle and Alexi had to lean against it to counter the weight. At the same time he heaved with all of his strength against the cord and pulled the Kolosh back to the surface.

He took hold of the Kolosh's hand and pulled it over the back deck of his baidarka. The Kolosh locked his fingers on the baidarka's frame and remained above the surface.

Alexi paddled for shore. The Kolosh was heavy, and progress was slow. His paddle bumped against the Kolosh and made holding a course difficult. Alexi worked like a madman and finally reached the shore. He rolled the baidarka away from the Kolosh and slid into the freezing water. The shock of the icy water squeezed the air from his lungs.

Stumbling, Alexi dragged the Kolosh onto the beach and stopped when his face was clear of the water. He untied the lanyard from his waist and pulled the boat up on the shore. The Kolosh was shaking violently, his body fighting the cold. Alexi grabbed the Kolosh by his arms and dragged him into the grass at the edge of the thicket.

Alexi returned to his baidarka and dug out his sleeping tarp and bundle of furs. The chill from the water was pushed from his mind as he raced to warm the Kolosh. He pulled the saturated deerskin jersey over the Kolosh's head and wrapped the furs around his bare torso, covering him with the canvas.

He went into the forest and started a fire. Alexi gathered an armload of branches and heaped them on the tiny flame. The fire smoldered, but soon bright yellow fingers reached up through the mound of spruce.

The Kolosh shook beneath the canvas tarp. His face was chalky, and Alexi feared he was too late. He dragged the shivering body through the thicket and into the woods near the fire. Flames leapt high into the air above the blaze. The heat stung Alexi's face as he moved the Kolosh nearer the fire. The warmth of the flames breathed new life into Alexi as he wrapped the Kolosh in the furs and canvas tarp.

The heat scorched his eyebrows, forcing him to move away. Alexi built a shelter over the Kolosh and draped the sailcloth tarp over it. The shelter served its purpose, and heat flowed over the Kolosh whose shaking had subsided. Alexi moved in close to the Kolosh's face. His breath came in ragged, wet gasps. There was little more he could do for the boy.

Alexi left to drag his baidarka into the tall grass and unpack his camp. The remainder of the day was spent watching the Kolosh and feeding the fire. He lunched on smoked salmon and berries he had gathered while collecting firewood. A small stream provided fresh water and he sprinkled some on the Kolosh's lips and forehead hoping to keep the sleeping boy alive.

The rain returned as night fell, and Alexi sat huddled in his damp clothes beside the fire, his coat wrapped tightly around his shoulders and one of the otter furs wrapped round his head and neck. His eyelids sagged over his tired eyes. Sleep crept into his cold body and tired brain.

The coals in the forge glowed white. The heat of a tiny sun poured from the firebox. The boy stood with his hands wrapped tightly around the bellows, lifting and then pulling down hard on the long handle that worked the ridges of the bag that forced air over the coals in the furnace. With heavy tongs, his father turned a long iron spike, holding it above the glowing coals. The spike was soon glowing bright red. His father withdrew the spike and laid it across a huge anvil. Plucking a heavy hammer from the bench, his father gently hammered the glowing piece of metal into a flat bar.

"More wind, more wind," his father urged as he plunged the piece of iron back into the furnace. The fire in the furnace crackled as small chips from the iron bar sprinkled down on the hot coals, sending a shower of sparks onto the thick leather apron that hung from his father's broad shoulders. His father smiled. His heavy black beard opened below his nose to reveal two bright rows of white teeth.

Alexi opened his eyes slowly and the dream turned to a nightmare. His father's smiling face had been replaced by that of a monster.

Shadowed against the glow from the fire, towered a menacing figure. A hideous face, streaked with black, and framed by a mass of bushy hair, stared down at him. A large ring pierced the nose of the monster and Alexi noticed a heavy club poised above the monster's shoulder. The club dropped suddenly and darkness exploded in a shower of stars.

Huna

Chapter 21

The dreams came many times and began to blend together. Sometimes he was helping his father in the foundry, then drinking tea and reading his lessons by the light of the candle at the small table in the cabin. In other dreams, he was hiding on the cliff, looking down upon the Kolosh women and children. Each dream would end the same. The monster loomed overhead. Glowing red eyes above a snarling mouth burnt holes into his chest and then the sky would fill with stars.

The smell of wood smoke and cooked fish pulled Alexi from sleep, and he lay for a long while, studying the smells. Freshly cut cedar released its sweet, oily scent. The smell of sweat and seal oil also came to him.

The sound of women speaking and children laughing seeped into Alexi's mind. The language was rough and came from deep in the throat. The voices moved nearer, then farther away, fading in and out. Alexi lay unmoving, sorting through the sounds. The feeling of his body joined the smells and sounds that swirled through his mind. One by one he wiggled his toes and fingers. He continued with his arms and legs, checking each part. Everything worked.

Alexi decided to open his eyes and take in his

surroundings. A heavy blanket pressed softly against his bare chest. He slowly opened his eyes, first only a small slit, and then he opened them wide. Everything was black. He moved a hand in front of his face but could see no sign of it in the blackness.

Panic gripped his chest. He could hear children laughing and moving some distance away, and the crackle of a fire came to him over the chatter. He used his fingers to make sure that his eyes were truly open. Nothing appeared.

Alexi wanted to shout out.

"Where am I? Why can't I see anything?" He screamed to himself.

Fear as he had never known flooded his chest. His heart raced and his skin was suddenly damp and hot. He explored the area beside him with his hands, careful not to move quickly for fear of drawing attention to himself. Beneath him he could feel a bed of animal hides, the soft hide curling easily under his touch.

He turned his head to one side and the explosion of pain made him instantly sick. He froze and waited for the pain to subside. After several minutes the nausea faded and the pain in his head became bearable.

He slid his hand toward his chin and slowly explored the right side of his face and head with his fingertips. The flesh was swollen, spongy and distorted. The slightest pressure brought warning of another wave of agony. He moved his hand away. Again he explored his face and found the right side of his head to be covered by a large, hard lump. The skin was stretched tight and the pain that emanated from his gentle touch was agony.

As he lay on his bed, willing the pain to leave his body, he felt a sensation of warmth on his shoulder and the left side of his face.

"Hello," he managed in a quavering voice. There was no reply, but he sensed someone was watching him.

"Hello, is anyone there?" He repeated the question and waited.

He heard quiet footsteps as his visitor scurried off. He strained his ears, and was surprised when the voices in the background stopped as one. Alexi could hear the crackle of a fire and a dog barking in the distance. A cold breeze swept across his body and he heard the approach of heavier footsteps. The steps grew louder and closer and stopped within arm's length of his head. Fear returned.

"Good day," a short greeting in Russian surprised Alexi.

"Where am I?" he asked.

"You are in the village of the Huna people, in the Shark House." Although the voice spoke Alexi's language, the speaker was not Russian.

Alexi lay silent, his mind working slowly. His aching head hindered his ability to think clearly. None of the other people he heard earlier spoke now.

"Am I a prisoner here?"

The visitor laughed, and then replied, "Far from a prisoner, you are an honored guest. The hit s'aati of the Shark house has worried every day that you would not awaken."

"How long have I been here?" Alexi inquired of his visitor.

"You were asleep for ten days," the reply shocked him.

"I have been here for ten days? How is that possible?"

"You were badly injured," the voice replied. "The shaman has tended your head and worked medicine on you. He will be pleased to know you have awakened."

"How was I injured?" Alexi asked, his painful head was a mystery, and his inability to see had not yet fully sunk in.

"It was a mistake," the visitor explained. He spoke slowly,

as if he were reaching for each word. "A search party was assembled to look for three boys that had taken a canoe for a seal hunt. They had been gone for two nights and their families grew worried. The hit s'aati of the Shark House is father to one of the boys."

The man paused. "They were searching the shore toward the Bay of Ice and found an overturned canoe. As nightfall approached they spotted the smoke from a fire. Expecting to find the boys warming themselves by the fire, the party advanced on the beach."

Alexi interrupted, "Was it my fire?"

"Ahh, you remember?" the visitor asked.

"A little, I remember a boy hanging onto a canoe," he said. "I helped him to the shore."

The memories came slowly, reforming in his aching head.

The visitor continued, "The search party found your kayak hidden in the grass and became wary. They approached your fire and discovered you sleeping beside the fire. The hit s'aati stole close to you while you slept and would have killed you had Wolf Boy not called out."

"What is a hit s'aati?" Alexi stopped his guest.

"Hit s'aati means headman, the head of the Shark House," his visitor explained.

"The hit s'aati, he hit me?" the vision of the monster flashed in his mind.

"Yes, but not a death blow. When he heard his son's voice, he broke his swing," his visitor explained. "The hit s'aati brought you back to the village with his son. He will be pleased that you have returned to the living."

The voices of children drew nearer and Alexi stopped to listen to their strange language.

"All of the children want to hear the story of the Russian hero," the visitor spoke, first in the language of the children and then to him in Russian.

"Why am I a hero?" Alexi asked.

"You saved the hit s'aati's only son," was the answer.

"The boy on the canoe was the hit s'aati's son?" Alexi asked.

"Yes,"

"What happened to the other boys?" He asked.

"They are gone," the visitor's voice trailed off. "The canoe was upset by strong currents. They all went into the water. Wolf Boy swam to the canoe but the other boys were swept away."

"This place, this village, it is a Kolosh village?" Alexi asked.

"To the Russians they are the Kolosh, but the people call themselves Tlingit," the visitor answered. The name started with the tongue pressed against the back of the teeth.

"Tlingit," Alexi repeated the name. "You are not one of them?"

"I am Unanga," he replied. "Your people call me Aleut."

"How do you know my language?" Alexi asked.

"When I was a boy I was taken by Russian hunters from my village on Unmak. I was taken to Kamchatka and trained in your language. The Russian hunters brought me to Alaska as a guide and interpreter. I was captured in a battle between the Tlingit and the Russians near the village of the Sit'ka people," the Unanga told his story. "The hit s'aati of the Shark House brought me to the village of the Huna. I have been with the people for seven winters."

"Did they harm you?" Alexi was curious.

"No, I am treated as member of the Shark House. I remember your language and help the hit s'aati trade with the Russians and English when their ships come."

"Ships, come here?" Alexi was excited.

"The Russians have taken the trade from the Huna people. We haven't traded with a ship in two seasons."

Alexi's spirits sank. Hope of a speedy return to New Archangel faded as quickly as it had appeared.

"I will leave now," the Unanga said. "You should sleep. The shaman will return soon and take praise for his success."

Alexi could hear his visitor as he moved away leaving only the whispers of the children behind.

Chapter 22

The shaman came to him as if in a dream. The shaman's bare feet swished as they slid along the floor. The thick scent of seal oil mingled with sweat and musty soil filled Alexi's nostrils. He wanted to cover his nose with his arm but didn't for fear of the pain. The shaman stopped beside him and murmured a slow chant. Alexi was calmed by the soft words. The shaman moved around his bed, chanting as he circled.

Alexi's eyes would not work and he shut them in anger. He turned his head to follow the shaman and pain flashed over him in a great wave. He saw spots of light against the blackness and waited as the pain faded. When he could once again focus, the shaman was gone. He longed for the chanting. It made him feel safe. He wondered if the shaman really had the power to heal him. Father Nikolai talked of the power of God to heal men and Alexi wondered if the shaman summoned the same God.

Alexi sensed the approach of someone different. His newest visitor smelled of the forest, spruce pitch and alder smoke. The approach was silent, but he could tell that someone stood nearby. What a strange sight he must be.

A soft voice, a young woman, spoke a few words he could not understand, and a warm hand closed around his. The woman guided his hand to a small bowl, which was warm to the touch. His hand closed around the bowl and the gentle hands urged him to lift the container to his lips. He realized that he was meant to drink from the bowl, but feared that if he moved his head the pain would once again surge through him.

The woman spoke again and placed her hand on his shoulder, pressing him firmly against the skins. Suddenly the bed beneath his back and shoulders began to rise. He was soon sitting up. The pain was mild. He lifted the dish to his lips, finding he had help as he did so.

The tea was strong and had the musty odor of devil's club. He sipped the bitter brew and winced at the taste. The woman spoke again and he felt her hands urging him to take another sip. He did so, and found it more bearable. He sipped the tea, pausing to let the taste fade from his mouth. When the tea was finished Alexi sank back into his bed, the warm hands took the bowl and the woman left.

Alexi opened his eyes, but saw only blackness. He quickly shut them and fell into a slumber.

When Alexi awoke next, he could sense the Unanga was near him. The smell of his clothes identified him.

"Hello," he said to the Unanga.

"Hello," the Unanga replied. "You are feeling better?"

"Yes, but I cannot see," Alexi said.

"You will see again when your head heals," was the Unanga's reply.

"I hope you are right," he said.

"You must sleep. Rest your head and heal your eyes," the Unanga suggested. "We will talk tomorrow."

"Wait," Alexi called to the Unanga as he moved away.

"Yes?" The Unanga replied.

Alexi asked, "What is your name?"

The Unanga paused. "My name among the Russians is Ivan. My name among the Unanga is Mush'kal."

"Thank you Mush'kal," Alexi replied and drifted again

into sleep.

Many days passed, and Alexi's head began to heal. The woman tended him and Mush'kal took him for short walks when he could stand the pain. The cool air smelled of dying leaves and seaweed. Mush'kal told him that the leaves had left the berry bushes and that the bears would soon be moving into the high country. It was the end of the gathering season and the village was making preparations for the coming snow. Alexi sensed the final weeks of the season but could no more see them than he could see the palm of his outstretched hand.

One morning, after the shaman had visited, he sat up on one elbow and listened to the sounds of the people of the house. He could identify the voices of ten children and knew many of them by their smell and the sound of their footsteps. They visited him daily, thinking that since he could not see them, he didn't know they were there.

The hit s'aati of the Shark House came and went many times each day, but never visited Alexi. The women were busy throughout the day, preparing meals and keeping the fire burning. The woman who tended him came with food when her family took their meals and Alexi learned to enjoy Tlingit food.

Salmon, halibut, seal and deer were eaten regularly, along with clams and other creatures gathered from the shore. Berries, roots, and wild rice provided sweet delight to complement the rich meats. Alexi marveled at the variety in the diet of the Tlingit.

One day Alexi opened his eyes to a gray and blurred haze. The distorted image startled him, but his heart leapt. He shut his eyes tightly. When he opened them again, the haze reappeared. It was dark and shadowed, but the shapes changed when he moved his eyes. He sank back on his bed and cupped his hands over his face. His vision was returning but he decided to keep it his secret.

The next morning the shapes were less blurred and brighter. He told no one of his improvement, but enjoyed watching the children as they moved around him, sneaking up to him and then slowly stealing away.

Mush'kal came to talk and Alexi told him his secret.

"I can see you today," Alexi announced without warning.

Mush'kal sat on a decorated box beside his bed. The box was painted in black with a magnificent bird. Eyes in the center of its wings stared at Alexi.

His friend bent close and looked into his eyes.

"Tell me what you see," Mush'kal demanded.

"I see the room and the women by the fire, I see the scars that decorate your cheeks," Alexi replied.

Mush'kal reached out a hand and took Alexi's shoulder, shaking him in pleasure.

"This is good news. Today you will meet the hit s'aati," Mush'kal took Alexi's arm, lifting him easily to his feet.

"Let us take a walk so that you may see the village," Mush'kal suggested.

Alexi followed his guide as they walked across the platform where his bed was located and ducked through the low door. He walked with Mush'kal down to a path in front of the Shark House.

The Shark House was long and wide. The planks that formed the walls stood side by side and had been smoothed with an adz. Each plank was held against the framework by wooden pegs and sinew lashings. The roof was also cut from planks and was covered with sheets of cedar bark.

The front of the house was painted in red, black and blue with the crests of the Shark house. Large figures were carved on the posts that supported the front of the long house. A bird with a sharp beak topped one pole, and the other was a man who held an octopus by the tentacles.

"What do the symbols mean?" Alexi asked Mush'kal.

"The hit s'aati can tell the story of his house," Mush'kal answered.

He walked Alexi along a path that followed the shoreline. A row of six long houses faced the ocean across the path. Several of the other houses were painted with figures. The Shark House was the last house at the eastern end of the village. The beach across the path was strewn with canoes of all shapes and sizes. Several large canoes were anchored away from the shore. Their high bows were painted with beautiful artwork. Alexi was certain they were war canoes.

A small island blocked the entrance to an inlet in front of the village. Alexi could see small totems and houses on the point of the island. A steep mountain rose behind the long houses. The bay in front of the village stretched away to the south. Tall mountains lined both sides of the bay, a fresh dusting of snow on the mountain tops shone bright in the sun. Beyond the last long house, a large cliff with a natural tunnel cut in the center offered a window into a large strait.

As the two walked through the village, people stared at Alexi. He wished he could make himself vanish.

Mush'kal smiled at him, "Everyone wishes to meet the boy who saved the hit s'aati's son."

"Where is the hit s'aati's son?" he inquired.

"He lives in the house of his uncle," Mush'kal explained. "Among the Tlingit, a boy is raised in the house of his mother's brother. Wolf Boy is hunting. You may meet him at the wedding."

"Wedding?" Alexi asked.

"The marriage of a nephew of the hit s'aati to a daughter of the Taku people," he answered.

"When is the wedding?" Alexi asked.

"Soon," Mush'kal replied.

Alexi nodded and continued to walk beside Mush'kal. He was weak and the ground was cold on his bare feet.

"Where is my baidarka?" he asked Mush'kal.

Alexi longed for his father and worried that he was suffering unneeded grief thinking that his son was dead. He had to get back as soon as possible.

"We shall go there now," Mush'kal answered, smiling. "It is a good kayak. You build it?"

"Yes, my father had a friend who hunted for the Company. An Aleut, er, Unanga like you," Alexi explained. "He helped me build it."

"I once had a kayak," Mush'kal recalled with sadness in his voice. "I have not paddled in many years."

"You may paddle my boat," Alexi offered.

"I am forbidden," Mush'kal informed him.

They arrived at a stand of spruce growing close to the water. The baidarka was suspended upside down beneath the branches of two trees. Alexi walked slowly around his boat, checking it for damage. He ran his hand over the taut skin. The baidarka was empty, his provisions and belongings had been removed.

"What has become of my long guns and furs?" Alexi asked Mush'kal as he studied his boat.

"They are stored in the Shark House," Mush'kal replied.

He found a single cracked rib and some small cuts in the tough hide covering. He could make the repairs easily and the boat would be ready to continue his voyage.

"How soon can I leave?" Alexi asked.

"Leave?" Mush'kal asked.

"Yes, I must go to New Archangel. My father must be very

worried," he explained.

"You can tell this to the hit s'aati, he will decide the time for your trip," Mush'kal said. He moved off down the path in the direction of the village. Alexi followed him.

Chapter 23

When they returned to the Shark House, Mush'kal left Alexi sitting on the cedar box next to his bed. His bed was in the corner of the house nearest the door. The inside walls of the long house were wide dimpled planks. Three large beams ran the length of the house and sat on sturdy poles spaced evenly along the length of the beams.

The floor was divided into three levels. A wide shelf that followed the walls around the inside of the house served as living quarters for the families who shared the house. A second, lower level formed a bench and was used as a gathering place during meals.

A third level had been dug down in the center of the house. In the center of the area, a fire pit provided for cooking and warmth for the house. A large hole in the ceiling allowed smoke to escape, though a thin blue haze hung in the air.

People took notice of Alexi. The woman who had tended him was busy at the fire. Two young girls brought her ingredients from containers spread around the fire pit.

Small rooms for each family, separated by woven screens, lined the upper platform along both sides of the house. An open area between Alexi's bed and the fire was the communal area where the men sat and talked in the evening hours. He had listened with great interest to their stories. Their laughter and applause made him long to understand their language.

A room at the back of the house was separated by a carved cedar screen the width of the house. Painted with a variety of animal figures, the screen was broken only by an oval shaped door at its center. This was the room of the hit s'aati and his family.

The woman tending the cooking made her way in his direction. She carried a wooden bowl and smiled as she approached. When she drew near, she waved her hand in front of his face. Alexi smiled. His secret was out. She spoke a few words and pushed the bowl in his direction. He took it and studied the contents. A stew of meat and seaweed steamed in the bowl. He thanked the woman and she returned to the fire.

As he ate the stew, Alexi studied the house carefully. In the ceiling above the central room, rows of spruce poles were draped with strips of smoked salmon. Above the partitioned rooms hung many masks, carved in animal forms and painted black and red. There were no men in the house. Alexi guessed they were out hunting.

Without warning, the shaman entered and everyone stopped what they were doing as he walked around the hearth. He stood very tall, taller than any man Alexi had seen in New Archangel. Thick, matted black hair hung below his waist. His face was a patchwork of tattoos and a large copper ring dangled from his nose. He would frighten the bravest of men. The shaman approached Alexi.

He walked around the boxes and Alexi's bed, reciting a different chant than on previous visits. The shaman shook a staff topped with a rattle. After making a few circles, the shaman stopped in front of Alexi and stopped chanting. He bent over and stared directly into Alexi's open eyes.

The shaman's eyes were a uniform black and Alexi felt as

though he could see into the man's head. The shaman reached out and took Alexi's head between his hands and looked into Alexi's eyes. After a moment, he released Alexi's head and walked to the door and was gone.

The woman returned for Alexi's bowl and smiled at him as she took her leave. Alexi sat on the box and wondered. Had the shaman truly cured him? It didn't matter how it had happened, having his sight back was the best thing that had ever happened and he was thankful.

The doorway to the house darkened again and the hit s'aati stepped into the room. He was followed by Mush'kal and three other men. The hit s'aati and Mush'kal approached Alexi and he stood to greet them.

The hit s'aati reached out for his arm. The powerful man grasped Alexi's elbow and hand and gave them a firm squeeze. The hit s'aati stepped back and spoke to him in Tlingit.

"He thanks you for saving his son," Mush'kal interpreted.

"I am grateful to him for sharing his home," Alexi replied.

"He is sorry for wounding you," Mush'kal summarized a lengthy speech.

"I have no ill feelings," Alexi said in reply.

Mush'kal translated and the hit s'aati nodded his head. The man who had once meant to kill him moved toward Alexi and gestured for him to move aside. As Alexi stepped back, the hit s'aati knelt and lifted a floorboard near Alexi's bed. Beneath the board was a long compartment. He could see his otter pelts, long guns, knife, pouch of shot, and fire tools neatly stacked in the space.

"Thank you," he said to whoever was listening as he bent down to gather his belongings. He tucked his fire tools into his pockets and then lifted one of the long guns. The rust from his voyage had been removed and a layer of fresh oil had been applied.

The hit s'aati spoke and Mush'kal translated.

"He asks how a young boy can own such fine long guns," Mush'kal translated.

"I saved them from the wreck of the ship I sailed on," Alexi answered. "I was stranded on an island on the coast many days ago. I was making my way to New Archangel when I was caught in a fog and terrible waters," Alexi continued. "Giant whirlpools tried to pull my boat under but I managed to escape. When the fog cleared I was surrounded by ice," Alexi spread his arms to emphasize the size of the icebergs.

Mush'kal translated and the hit s'aati laughed and made stirring motions with his hands.

"He says you are lucky to have lived," Mush'kal said. "The channels through the islands are very dangerous. Only experienced men travel those passages."

"I am fortunate," Alexi said.

"And what of the others on your ship?" the hit s'aati asked.

"They abandoned the ship before it hit the rocks. I and one other person were trapped aboard and came ashore with the boat. The other man was already dead. The mast of the ship crushed him," Alexi summarized his misfortune.

"You wish to travel to the Russian Fort?" the hit s'aati confirmed Alexi's plan.

"Yes, yes I do, as soon as I can get provisions and directions," Alexi replied.

There was a long pause and the hit s'aati looked past Alexi, then looked him up and down, cocking his head from side to side to take full measure of him.

"He says you must wait until the snows begin to leave before making that voyage."

Alexi was concerned when Mush'kal suggested he would remain at the village.

"Tell him I must go as soon as possible. My father is waiting," Alexi's tone grew urgent.

The hit s'aati launched into a long speech, using his hands to keep his audience focused. When he was finished, Mush'kal translated.

"If you leave now, you will be swallowed by the waves in the passes to the ocean. If you choose the trade route, you will need guides and protection against the other clans. The men are busy hunting for the winter and a guide cannot be spared to protect you."

Mush'kal continued, "The hit s'aati says the people of the Shark House will journey to the Sit'ka when the herring spawn. You will be his guest until then."

The hit s'aati turned away and moved toward the fire, joining a group of small children and women tending their cooking.

Mush'kal stayed with Alexi.

"Does this mean I am a prisoner?" Alexi asked.

"Not a prisoner. A guest who is expected to stay a while longer," Mush'kal smiled. Two of his front teeth were missing. "If you leave, you will insult the hit s'aati and the people of the village. This is not a good thing. It is dangerous to travel alone through the lands of the Tlingit."

Alexi sagged onto the box, angry with the hit s'aati. *His father was suffering great sadness thinking his only son was drowned.*

"I will risk the trip if the hit s'aati can make me a map of the trade route," Alexi persisted. "I have provisions and I can take care of myself."

"The hit s'aati has spoken on this," Mush'kal repeated his earlier message. "You will stay."

Alexi's shoulders slumped and he bowed his head. Tears welled in his eyes but he bit his lip and fought them back. He couldn't think clearly. The hope that he would see his father before the snow came faded like a dying candle.

"Come with me now and we will get your kayak into the water," Mush'kal suggested, trying to stir his young friend from his sadness.

Alexi rose and followed Mush'kal. He and Mush'kal spent the better part of the afternoon repairing the baidarka. Mush'kal was expert with a needle and the boat soon looked as good as when new. The two of them sat on the shore, enjoying the cool breeze as they watched the flocks of geese and ducks high in the sky making their way south. Alexi longed for a pair of wings.

Chapter 24

In the days that followed, Alexi settled into life in the Shark House. Mush'kal and other men who had been captured spent the days collecting firewood. They built more racks for the smoked deer and seal meat that was brought in by the hunters. Preparations were being made for the wedding and everyone in the house was busy.

In the evenings the people danced and sang songs, practicing for the upcoming event. The costumes and animal masks used in the dance intrigued Alexi. The elder men and women in the house spent many hours reciting the stories of the Huna people. Mush'kal translated for Alexi.

Alexi thought constantly about his father and New Archangel.

On a sunny morning, one of the children of the Shark House dove through the door shouting an alarm. People got to their feet and removed their garments from cedar boxes and spoke excitedly amongst themselves. Alexi went out of the house.

The people of the Shark House gathered on the shore and trained their eyes on the water to the west of the village.

Soon, three canoes appeared from behind the cliff. The middle canoe carried many people. A man stood in the bow holding a staff. As the canoes drew closer, the people of the Shark House began to sing to the steady beat of a drum. It was a song Alexi recognized from the nights around the fire.

The song grew louder as the canoes approached.

People from a house at the other end of the village also wore bright costumes. Dressed in blankets and carved masks, they were an awesome sight. Others from the village watched from the shore but were not specially dressed.

Mush'kal stood beside Alexi.

When the canoes were a stone's throw from the shore, the Shark House stopped their song and the people in the canoe stopped. The man in the bow of the largest canoe shouted and the hit s'aati of the Shark House shouted a reply. The man in the canoe made a long speech. The children stood silent, gazing intently at the visitors in the three canoes.

Suddenly the people in the canoes broke into song. Chanting and drumming, they returned the song given them by the people on the shore. When the song was finished, the hit s'aati made a final speech and the canoes came ashore.

The people of the Shark House moved forward to help land the canoes. At the same time, the rest of the costumed people moved down the path and joined the others. The visitors piled out of the canoes and mixed with the people of the Huna village. The men spent a great deal of time greeting their guests. Stories were being told, Alexi could tell.

The hit s'aati of the Shark House spoke some forceful words to the visitors and they all turned their eyes toward Alexi. Alexi suddenly felt out of place, the way he had often felt at the school in New Archangel when Father Nikolai had singled him out for praise.

Then the eyes of the group turned to a young man from the other house. The young man stared at Alexi, his eyes piercing. Alexi was frightened by the look.

"That is Wolf Boy," Mush'kal whispered. "You are now a hero in their village, for you saved one of their clan from the Kushtakah," He translated the speech.

"I don't like being a hero," Alexi said.

Mush'kal laughed.

A group of small boys ran toward him and took his hands in admiration. The children all spoke at one once and Alexi could little understand anything they said, but could tell from their excitement they wanted something.

"They want to hear the story of how you saved Wolf Boy," Mush'kal explained their chatter.

"They will have to wait for that story," Alexi answered and smiled at the boys as he walked toward the canoes to help unload. The people mingled on the beach, catching up on the news of one another's villages and renewing old friendships.

When the canoes were unloaded, the Taku people entered the long house to set up housekeeping. The celebration would begin at sundown and everyone was busy with preparations.

When the celebration began, food was served to the guests by members of the Shark House. Portions of smoked salmon and deer meat were heaped on their guest's platters.

Speeches were given and the people listened to each with equal interest. The feasting and speaking went on late into the night.

The following morning the house was awake with the sun. The weather was fine and the morning was spent singing songs and racing canoes. While the men paddled, the people shouted encouragement from the shore. The racing and singing carried on until the sun was at its highest.

After the races, the people retired into the house and began a feast that lasted into the night. The hit s'aati of the Taku people was given many fine gifts of furs and carved masks by the hit s'aati of the Shark House.

Furs, blankets, copper medals, food and many carved

objects were presented to the guests. Between the gift giving, people stood and gave speeches and sang songs, each clan taking its turn in response to the previous presentation.

Huge amounts of fish and meat were eaten. The women carried baskets of herring eggs and boxes of seal oil, offering them to the guests first and then to the members of their own house. Everyone was having a great time and the children ran among the crowd, stealing morsels of food and listening to the fantastic stories.

Alexi wandered in and out of the house during the three days of the celebration. He was restless, and felt very alone. Mush'kal was kept busy and had little time to translate the speeches and songs.

The other houses of the village went about their business as if nothing were happening.

Alexi sat each day on a log high on the hill behind the village and watched as the canoes came and went. On one occasion he saw a group of men bring in the bodies of seven seals. The speed with which the men skinned and cut up the seals made him feel foolish at having taken two full days in his efforts. He learned from watching them, and would do better the next chance he had.

His strength had returned, and he was ready to venture out in his baidarka. He walked out onto the point beyond the last house. Alexi carried his fire making tools and knife as he made his way to the stand of trees where his baidarka hung. Mush'kal had called it a kayak. Alexi had taken a liking to the shorter name.

The oil on the kayak was fresh and the skin taut. The boat slid easily from its stand and Alexi set it on the ground beside him. He fitted the grass mat and lifted the kayak over his shoulder and carried it to the water. Once away from the shore, the tension melted from his body. The cries of the birds on the shoreline calmed his mind.

Alexi explored the shoreline to the west of the tunnel.

The shoreline curved to the north as Alexi moved away from the village and the small bay opened up into a strait that was five leagues across. Scattered on the expanse of water were white hulks of floating ice. The mountains on the distant shore dwarfed those behind the village, and they were covered by a thick blanket of snow.

Alexi drifted, riding along on the tide as he surveyed the hills behind the village and a group of islands on the shore opposite the village. Bear Bay was three leagues across and the mirror-like water reflected the mountains on the far side.

His arms quickly tired and his legs grew stiff. He turned back toward the village.

When he approached the shoreline, a group of small boys rushed down the shoreline to help him land his kayak. They ran their hands over the oily skin and chattered noisily amongst themselves. When Alexi had pulled himself free of the small boat, they took up the ends, hoping to carry the boat up the beach. Alexi laughed and took hold of the bow, motioning for the boys to take the stern. Together, they carried the kayak up beyond the mounded seaweed that marked the highest tide. The boys scurried off to pursue a squirrel that had caught their attention.

The sun was nearly down on the third day of the celebration. Alexi turned the skin boat over and returned to the Shark House.

The dancing and singing was over and the guests were making preparations for departure. Mush'kal met him at the door.

"The Taku people will return to their village tomorrow," Mush'kal explained to Alexi. "The shaman predicts bad weather so they will race the storm."

"How far is their village?" Alexi asked his translator and new friend.

"Three day's journey," Mush'kal replied.

That evening, the people of both houses sat in small groups eating fish, berries and seaweed and talking about the recent events. Alexi lay in his bed listening to the people and missing his father. He fell asleep to the sound of the confusing tongue.

Chapter 25

In the days following the visit from the Taku people, the people of the Shark House worked to rebuild their food stores. The celebration had depleted the fish and deer supply. With winter approaching the Shark House had much to gather.

The men went hunting every day for seal, deer and waterfowl while the women collected shellfish and seaweed.

Alexi spent most of his time picking what few berries could be found on the bushes near the village with the younger children. He was permitted to carry his long gun and served as both a protector and extra pair of hands. The season was late, but there had not yet been a hard freeze. The berries were ripened to perfection.

One morning, the men of the Shark House set out in the canoes to hunt seals in the Bay of Ice. When the men had gone, Alexi was left with the youngest of the children. They decided to make an outing into the forest to fill two cedar boxes with berries, dividing into two smaller parties to see who could fill their box first.

The berry pickers hiked into the forest before settling in a thick patch of the ripe berries. The contest was started and soon both groups were collecting berries as fast as they could. Suddenly, a large brown shape reared up at the edge of the berry patch and gave several loud and low woofs. Everyone froze and stared at the bear towering over the bushes.

One of the littlest girls screamed and started running. The bear startled at the sound and dropped to all fours and charged in the direction of the scream. Alexi had little time to act and in a flash shouldered his long gun and let fly a shot in the direction of the bear. The ball missed its mark, but the loud noise turned the bear and it vanished into the thick brush as suddenly as it had appeared.

The children stared after the bear for several moments. They turned as one and rushed toward Alexi, hugging him around his waist and shouting.

The children were joyful but Alexi was shaking. They gathered the boxes, which were not filled, and headed down the hill after the girl who had fled. They found her in the Shark House hiding under a pile of blankets. They enticed her to the fire with a few handfuls of berries.

The women were excited by the story of the encounter with the bear and they teased Alexi through his interpreter. He blushed and left the house.

Alexi went for a paddle to the east of the village. The beach became very gradual and a large grassy flat formed by a small river filled a gap between the village and another peninsula.

The water was calm, and the chill in the air was kept at bay by his new fur hat. The hit s'aati of the Shark House had presented him with the hat during the wedding celebration. The otter fur lining was soft against his head and kept him overly warm. The hat was shaped like a bowl and covered the top of his ears. The outer shell of the hat was made from tanned deerskin and was supple and waterproof. Alexi was proud of the hat and wore it every day.

He spent the day walking on the islands and exploring several long sloughs that ran deep into the forest.

Ten days after their departure, the hunters returned in the canoes and the whole village poured from their houses to greet them. The men had taken thirty seals, ten deer, five geese, and a pile of black seabirds.

The house was busy for days preparing and storing the game the men had brought back. The seal oil was stored in cedar boxes. The flesh of the deer and seals was stripped and smoked. The racks in the rafters of the Shark House once again grew full.

Mush'kal informed Alexi that the snow salmon would soon return and the people of the Shark House would feast on the prized fish. Soon a few salmon were seen jumping in the bay in front of the village. Many of the house members left with supplies for a fish camp, and were gone four days. They returned in a canoe loaded with strips of smoked salmon. The fish were stored with the rest of the meats, and the fishermen returned to the stream.

As Alexi grew comfortable with life in the village, he was invited into the houses of the other clans to share meals and tell the story of the shipwreck and his journey to the village. Mush'kal became his constant companion, as he needed him to translate. He also learned many words of the Tlingit language, but it was a difficult language and his progress was slow.

Alexi noticed that Wolf Boy avoided him. It was as if Alexi did not exist to the young Tlingit whom he had saved from drowning.

Before the fish-camp party had returned a second time, snow came. The first snow was heavy and wet, and was quickly rained away. The Tlingit moved their lives inside and ventured out for hunting only when the weather was favorable.

As winter settled in, the people gathered more food from

the shore. Delicious clams and cockles were available whenever the tide was out. They were steamed in boxes with hot rocks. The boiling water opened their shells making it easy to pull the tasty flesh out for eating. The empty shells formed a mound beside the house.

When the snow reached the water's edge, travel along the shore became difficult. The narrow path that wound through the village was the only easy walking. The snow had reached knee deep, and walking in the forest was difficult. The deer moved to the shore to feed on the grasses buried under the snow and the bears were in their winter dens.

Early one morning, after a heavy snow, Wolf Boy finally showed himself in the Shark House. He was accompanied by two other young men. They entered the house and were invited by the wife of the halibut fisherman to have a bowl of tea to warm them. The visitors accepted the offer and asked Alexi to join them. Mush'kal sat with him as they sipped their tea.

Soon the visitors turned their attention to Alexi. They asked him a question which Mush'kal translated. "These three young men invite you to join them in their canoe for a deer hunt," He explained. "They will be gone for one day and will scout the shoreline for feeding deer."

"Am I to bring my long gun?" Alexi asked.

Mush'kal spoke to the three and Wolf Boy answered him with gestures and a speech.

"He says they will be hunting with lances."

"Will we leave now?" Alexi asked.

Mush'kal said they would leave right away.

The trio left and Alexi went to collect his things for the hunt. He pulled on a deerskin shirt that he had been given by the hit s'aati's wife. He put on his otter hat and moose hide boots he had traded from one of the men in the Shark House.

He gathered some fish and dried seaweed into a canvas bag and collected his canvas coat from the box by his bed. Alexi tucked his fire tools and knife into his pockets and made his way to the door.

Mush'kal stopped him at the door and looked into his face.

"Be careful around Wolf Boy," he cautioned. "He envies the favor you are shown by the hit s'aati."

"Surely he knows I don't hold a grudge against him," Alexi replied to Mush'kal.

"He has no concern for what you feel. His shame for having failed to prove his manhood burns in his chest and you remind him of the failure. The hit s'aati has noticed these things," Mush'kal explained. "Be careful Alexi," Mush'kal gripped his forearm and stood aside to let him pass.

The young men waited on the shore beside a floating canoe. Alexi made his way down the slippery path to join them.

Chapter 26

The waters of Bear Bay were as smooth as a looking glass and reflected the white blanket of snow that smothered the mountains. The four young men paddled in unison, and soon disappeared behind the island in front of the village.

The canoe moved easily along the shore as the boys scanned the beaches for signs of their quarry. They traveled a league before one of the boys made gestures and words pointing to the shoreline across the bay. The others nodded agreement and they turned the canoe to a heading which would carry them across the bay to the mouth of a long inlet. The paddlers were winded when they entered the inlet on the other side of the bay.

Once in the inlet, they moved close to shore and rested. The village had long since disappeared from sight.

While they scanned the beach for signs of deer, Wolf Boy opened a wooden box and removed strips of smoked fish. He passed the fish to Alexi and the others in the boat and they all sat and chewed the smoky flesh while they drifted. The crisp air felt good on Alexi's face.

The boy in the front of the canoe pointed to the shore and they all noticed three sets of tracks cutting across the snow between the water and the alder thicket. They paddled to shore and landed on the beach. They pulled the canoe clear of the water and lashed it to a tree.

Wolf Boy pulled four lances out of the bow of the canoe

and handed them out. They were made from sturdy spruce poles and the points had been hardened in a fire. Alexi had tossed a lance in the village but as he had long guns hadn't taken much time to practice with the spear. It would be exciting to kill a deer at close quarters.

Wolf Boy made signs that Alexi was to accompany the younger of the other two boys and hunt higher on the hillside. Wolf Boy and the other boy would move through the woods near the shore.

Alexi followed his companion into the woods, wading through snow that reached to his knees. Once they entered the tall timber, the snow was harder and patches of open ground could be found close to the trees. Alexi and his companion followed the tracks that led from the beach. They stopped frequently and the Tlingit blew a deer call. The call was made from a small piece of wood slit its full length. Between the pieces of the stick was a blade of grass. When the hunter blew on the call, the sound of a bleating fawn echoed through the empty forest.

The Tlingit suddenly stopped and pointed ahead. He held his hand beside his head with two fingers pointing up. Alexi knew he had spotted a buck deer and the stalk would begin. The Tlingit hefted his lance and made a sign for Alexi to circle higher on the hill to scare the animal down to him. Alexi nodded and made his way as quietly as possible up the steep slope. His heart pounded in his ears.

When he thought he was high enough, Alexi followed the hillside and made his way along the ridge. He could see glimpses of the water far below and the strip of snow covered beach through the trees. After a bit, he began to work his way down the hill. As he got closer to the shore, he was puzzled that he had not heard or seen the other hunters. He broke out of the forest onto the shore, hoping to see one of the other boys. The shore was empty.

Tired and wet, Alexi made his way toward the canoe to await the return of the other hunters. He ate his fish and seaweed as he walked along the shore looking for the canoe, but was unable to find it. He turned anxiously to scan the water. Perhaps the tide had taken the boat and it had drifted away. Nothing floated in the inlet but birds and seaweed.

Alexi's skin flashed hot when he realized what had become of the other boys. He had been abandoned, Mush'kal had been right to warn him.

The deer tracks, which had drawn them to the shore, were still there, as were his and the other boy's tracks. He walked down the shoreline and discovered a single set of tracks leaving the thicket where the canoe had been moored. A little further on, two sets of footprints entered the forest. Alexi followed the tracks only to find them double back toward the canoe.

The game had been beautifully played. He had not been harmed, but with no provisions and a cold night setting in, the three boys had left him for dead.

As light began to fade, Alexi gathered firewood. He broke dead dry branches from under a wind fallen tree and built a shelter against a steep bank inside of the tree line. He cut an armful of small hemlock boughs with his knife and made a thick pile under the shelter. The boughs would be his mattress and his blanket. He built a small fire near the mouth of the shelter and went to the beach.

The tide was low, and Alexi dug in the mud with a driftwood stick. In a short time he had turned up a dozen clams. He cleared a spot amongst the coals and placed his dinner over the embers.

As the heat penetrated the hard white clam shells, they slowly opened, revealing the pink flesh inside. Alexi removed the sizzling clams from the fire and let them cool on the snow. They made a fine dinner.

He piled large pieces of dry spruce on the fire and buried himself in his bed of boughs. He was cold but slept a little, waking frequently to feed the fire.

Bear Bay

Chapter 27

At first light Alexi shivered from under the branches and stoked his fire. A light snow was falling and the forest and water were silent. The ripples left by a pair of seabirds were the only imperfections on the water.

He was far from the village, a walk of how many days he didn't know. He could find plenty of food on the shore. Clams, crabs and seaweed would sustain him. Without a boat he could hardly cross the bay to the village. He remembered conversations with Mush'kal about the length of Bear Bay and how it narrowed to a fine channel near the end. He would walk to the end of the bay and the full length of the opposite shore to reach the village. He set out immediately.

The beach was gentle and walking was easy as he made his way up the inlet. By midday he reached a wide flat of grass-covered mud. Midway across the flat he encountered a wide stream. He forded it with ease, but was soaked to the waist when he reached the opposite shore.

His wet trousers and the chilly air set him to shivering. He hurried to the forest and built a fire to dry off. He had saved a few clams from the night before, and ate them while steam rose from his soggy breeches.

The winter sun set quickly. Alexi made camp and hunted among the rocks for his dinner. He ate two small crabs that he found hidden under the matting of grass. He slept cold in a nest of boughs.

At first light he made his way out onto the flats and studied the country. The hills that lined the inlet were low and stretched far inland before rising to tall mountains. As he explored deeper into an arm of the flats he spotted the frames of several shelters. Hoping to find something he might use on his journey, he approached the abandoned camp. As he searched the fish camp, he spotted a bundle hanging high in a tree. He scaled the tree and cut it down.

The bundle was a mat of woven spruce root. He rolled it open, and discovered a small axe and spoon carved from a sheep's horn. The mat and axe would be very useful and he was happy to have found them. He rolled them back together and continued down the shore. The lance made a good walking stick and helped steady him when he had to cross slippery rocks and snow.

Alexi had to skirt around two more deep inlets. When he emerged from the last inlet, he could see to the mouth of the bay. A faint cloud of smoke hanging over a tiny spot on the shore many leagues away marked the village. He made his bed under a tree and slept.

The next day snow fell in wet sheets driven by gusty winds. He remained camped at the foot of the mountain. He scanned the bay for signs of a search party, but saw none. The storm grew more intense and he added another layer of boughs. He rested comfortably wrapped in the mat buried in the pile of boughs. The heat from the fire reflected from the roof of his shelter and at times he was too warm. To pass the time, he carved a bowl from a burl he had hewn from a spruce the day before.

Chapter 28

After two days the storm passed and the glow of a bright sun peered over the mountains. Across the bay, golden streaks banded the mountain tops and the windswept peaks jutted from the white blanket like gray daggers.

It was much colder and Alexi kept his hands jammed deeply into his pockets as he shuffled along the rocky shore. As he moved deeper into Bear Bay the far shore drew closer. At the base of a steep mountain the gap was at its narrowest, then widened greatly. The shore was no more than two hundred paces distant.

The narrows provided a dilemma for Alexi. Crossing the narrow passage would cut many days from his journey. If he risked a crossing he might tire and drown. If he kept walking the shoreline, he would face many more cold nights.

Alexi paced back and forth along the shore, studying the stretch of water and the materials at hand. Needing to rest, he sat on a log and pondered his problem. From the woods behind him he heard a strange chirping mixed with low growls.

Suddenly a land otter burst out of the thicket a few paces from him. The otter slunk toward the water, its long back arching high with each step. When it reached the water's edge, the otter turned and looked directly at Alexi. The otter's black eyes seemed wise. Alexi watched as the otter slipped beneath the surface.

Alexi scanned the water for a sign of his visitor and finally spotted the animal half way to the far shore. The otter swam the remaining distance on the surface. When the otter emerged on the far shore it shook the water from its sleek brown fur and turned to face Alexi who sat motionless. The otter held Alexi's glance for only a moment and then disappeared into the thicket. Alexi decided he too would cross.

He searched the edge of the alders and found a piece of driftwood he judged large enough to carry his weight. He cut a spruce pole and trimmed its limbs. Using the pole as a lever, he worked the log free of its entanglement and rolled it down to the water. When the log reached the water, it sank almost out of sight. The driftwood log was barely visible above the water, and could be pushed under easily. He would have to cut a fresh tree.

Walking along the shore he selected a spruce the diameter of his body and set upon it with his axe. The spruce was hard and by the time the sun was gone, he had cut through less than one third of the trunk. He set up camp and rested by his fire, dining on clams and bits of seaweed. The bitter cold oozed in around him and he shivered through the night under his mat and pile of boughs in spite of a roaring fire.

By midday the next day, Alexi had felled the tree. Its top branches stretched well out into the water. He removed the limbs and cut the trunk to twice his height. It took another day to finish his raft, and his hands were badly blistered for his efforts. Many times he flopped exhausted beside his fire and lay there while his strength and spirit were slowly refreshed by the flames.

The third morning in his camp, Alexi used the pole to pry his log to the water's edge. He had left two short limbs sticking out to tie on another thick branch for extra support. He had seen a sketch of a canoe used by the people in the Sandwich Islands; the outrigger gave the canoe stability. Using spruce roots pulled from his sleeping mat, he lashed a short log to the limbs and stood back to examine his craft. It would do. He had shaped a crude paddle from a limb.

When the tide reached the lowest point of the day, he lashed his belongings to the front of the log and pushed his raft into the water. The icy water soaked through his boots and trousers, biting at his flesh. Alexi sucked in a deep breath and held it as he entered the water. The water reached his waist as he straddled the log in the shallow water. He leaned forward over his bundle, and pushed away from the shore. The log hesitated for a moment, dragging on the bottom. Balancing his weight on the side where the outrigger was lashed, he started paddling.

It reminded him of paddling the beam to the *Irena*. The water quickly numbed his legs and his body began to shake. By the time he was midway to the far shore, his strength had begun to ebb and he fought to concentrate on paddling. After what seemed an eternity, the end of his log bumped against the shore. He mustered all of his strength to climb off. His feet slipped and he stumbled in the shallow water, landing on his back.

Panic gripped Alexi, losing his strength might prove fatal. He crawled out of the water, cut the lashings on his bundle and dragged it up the shore. He made his way into the forest and searched out some dry moss. His legs were throbbing. He gathered several handfuls of moss and tucked them under a bundle of dry spruce twigs. The flint and steel shook badly in his frozen hands and he had difficulty bringing them together. With tears of frustration welling in his eyes, a shower of sparks leapt into his tinder and an ember was born.

He fed the flame small spruce twigs and it grew to a crackling blaze. He knelt by the fire, letting the warmth sweep over him. When he had stopped shaking, he unrolled his spruce mat and stripped out of his wet clothes. He huddled close to the fire with his mat wrapped round his shoulders, using it to direct the heat over his body. Little by little feeling returned to his skin and frozen legs.

His shivering subsided and he could again think clearly. His soggy boots and clothes steamed on the ground by the fire. He turned them often to dry them evenly.

When his clothes were dried, he slipped into the warm garments and boots and stretched. The sun was gone, replaced by the faint glow of the winter twilight. He walked to the beach and collected some seaweed to chew for dinner. The coldest air of the winter settled over the bay as he gathered in a thick pile of boughs for his bed.

His empty stomach tortured him through the night and the cold stabbed at every exposed patch of skin. He slept little and sat tending his fire at first light. The tide was out so Alexi scavenged a meal of clams and enjoyed the chewy morsels cooked in the coals.

He built a thicker shelter against a growing wind and spent the day exploring around his camp and resting. Several deer trails cut through the thicket near his camp. There were plenty of fresh tracks and he hatched a plan to get a meal of venison. He practiced throwing the lance at short distances, driving the hard point into the crusty snow. He doubted any deer would come within a league of him. He smelled of sweat and smoke, but he would give the hunt his best effort.

In the light of the early morning he climbed a thick spruce that overhung a well-worn trail. Alexi perched on a low branch just above the trail, poised to strike. His muscles ached and the branches wore into his cold feet and arms. He shifted his weight constantly, rubbing his hands and feet to keep them warm in the bitter air. As the midday sun passed behind the mountain, a lone deer came into view. The small animal appeared unhealthy and paid little attention as it plodded along the shore, following the trail toward the thicket. Alexi's heart raced.

The deer hesitated, testing the air with a quivering nose. Alexi's breath caught in his chest. The deer bent to the trail and sniffed the snow, backing away. Disappointment swept over Alexi. Would he come so close and fail? Suddenly the deer straightened and moved forward. Alexi had little time to react and dropped from his perch as the deer passed below. The point of the lance pierced the deer's back behind its shoulders. His weight drove the shaft through the deer's lungs before sticking deep in the trail. The deer struggled for a moment and then fell limp.

Alexi lay on the ground beside his prize. His heart pounded and he struggled to catch his breath. He yelled at the top of his lungs though no one would hear. The fresh wound steamed in the cold air as did the pool of blood that oozed from beneath the deer's body. He pulled the lance out and rolled the deer onto its side. The deer was thin but not starving. Winter had taken its toll on the young doe but there was plenty of meat on the body.

He set about dressing the animal. The deer's flesh warmed his hands as he worked with his knife. By day's end he had stripped the flesh from the bones and piled it on the deer's hide beside his fire.

Alexi enjoyed a delicious slice of meat, roasted over the coals. The hot juices ran from the corners of his mouth, dripping onto the front of his jersey. The life he had taken from the deer replenished his strength and he slept without noticing the cold.

With the sun's appearance he wrapped most of the meat in the deer's hide. The rest would feed the ravens and other forest animals. Alexi carried the bundle of meat slung over his shoulder. He used his lance as a walking stick as he made his way along the rocky shoreline.

Chapter 29

As Alexi moved away from his camp, the walking became easier. The sharp and uneven rocks that covered the shoreline gave way to small, rounded stones. In the distance he could see a large tidal flat that stretched two leagues. At the edge of the flat, a stream blocked his way. Alexi dreaded being wet again and decided to walk upstream to find a suitable crossing.

Several hundred paces up the stream bank a series of rocks made a natural path across the clear water. He hopped across the rocks and soon trudged through knee-deep snow on the opposite shore. With dry clothes and a satisfied appetite, he was enjoying the time alone. The sunny weather made him feel good. The beauty of the mountains and the mirror of the bay helped take his mind off his struggle and he pushed on at a strong pace.

Several long rocky points turned out from the beach and Alexi cut through the forest on each of them. Doing so shortened the journey but wading through the deep snow drained his energy.

The sun set out of a clear sky and the temperature dropped even further. His breath formed clouds of white as he scouted for a suitable campsite. A full moon shone brightly. He chose a spot beneath an overhanging bank and dug a small cave into the snow that had drifted below the bank. He built a fire in front of the cave and cut limbs for his bed.

He unrolled his bundle of meat and set the frozen strips on the snow beside the fire. He cut four limbs and fashioned a frame over which he stretched the deer hide, propping it near the fire to dry. He dined on fresh venison, savoring each bite. Before turning in for the night, he spread the dry deer hide on the floor of his cave and piled the hemlock boughs high over his spruce root mat.

As he listened to the crackling fire a loud hooting echoed through the forest. The sound grew nearer and more frequent until it was coming from a tree directly over his cave. Alexi enjoyed the company. The owl hooted a melancholy song in the darkness and Alexi found himself thinking of his father. He slept little as the cold bit at his feet and hands. He passed time stoking the fire and huddling under his cover as he watched the cold moon pass overhead. He longed for the warm quilts he had burrowed under on the cold nights in New Archangel. The warm hearth of the Shark House would be welcome when he completed his journey.

The dark of the night sky with its speckling of stars slowly faded to pink twilight. Alexi rose, ate some venison, and melted snow in his wooden bowl. The bitter cold decided for him that he would stay in camp. When the weather warmed, traveling would be more comfortable. He spent the next four days snacking on roasted venison. He improved his shelter and banked his fire pit to send more of its heat over his bed and slept more comfortably each night. In the late evening of the fifth day in the camp, the stars blinked out slowly as a blanket of clouds poured in from the west. The air warmed quickly and the frost that had formed on the rocks and trees melted away. By morning a steady drizzle had replaced the frigid air.

Alexi packed his camp and the remaining venison and

headed down the shore. Across Bear Bay he could see the inlet in which he had been abandoned. Although there were still rivers and marshes to cross, he knew he was nearing the village.

Through the day he crossed two small streams and a river. The river was covered with ice thick enough to walk on. The rain turned to light snow as evening fell. He thought he might reach the village within a day.

The shoreline had become a series of inlets that cut into the low hills above the beach. The small bay he faced was dotted with rock piles and small islands. As he scouted for an area to camp, he discovered a plank hut near the mouth of a stream, a fish camp. The hut had a dirt floor and large gaps between the planks. There was a small hearth in the center of the hut and a hole in the roof to let out the smoke. He used his last square of char cloth to bring a fire to life and cooked half of the remaining venison.

The shelter was a welcome break from the cold ground and Alexi slipped into a deep sleep.

The boy was far from shore on the deck of a giant ship. As far as the eye could see in every direction, seabirds swarmed and squawked. Schools of herring boiled on the surface, pursued by masses of hungry salmon. Eagles swooped down to snag the unsuspecting fish. The ship bobbed gracefully on the gentle swells, her full sails stretched taut by a steady wind.

The sound of dripping water woke Alexi from his dream. The heat from his fire had melted the snow on the roof and water trickled through the cracks. It was still dark and he felt for water on his bed, but his mat was dry. He poked the coals back to life and stoked his fire. The flames that licked at the limbs he added cast dancing shadows on the walls and ceiling. He slipped back to his dreams.

The final day of the journey passed slowly as a thick fog had settled over the bay. The snow had stopped and the air was cool. He took his bearings from the faint sun that oozed through the fog.

By mid-morning he stood on the bank of a large river. The warm weather had thawed the ice and it was too thin to cross. Leads of open water were visible as far as he could see upstream. He wanted to stay dry so he picked his way through the forest, walking on the hard crust of snow. The snow crunched under his feet. He reached a large tree that had fallen across the river. The mass of roots torn from the earth reached skyward like the gnarled fingers of an old witch.

Alexi picked his way between the limbs until he stood on the opposite shore. The burial totems on the island in front of the village soon came into view and he felt a wave of relief and then a knot in his stomach. Many days had passed since he had been abandoned and he wondered how he would be received. He had rehearsed the story he would tell many times as he lay huddled in his bed.

As midday came to pass, the fog lifted and the Huna village appeared. Scattered clouds littered a dark blue sky and the sun shone brightly on the fresh snow. The village was quiet, the canoes were lined up on the beach and a few dogs chased each other, weaving among the canoes. Smoke rose lazily above the roofs of each of the long houses settling over the village.

As Alexi approached the Shark House two small boys tumbled onto the porch. They wrestled for a moment and froze when they saw Alexi. Before Alexi could raise a tired arm to greet them they dived back into the house.

Soon Mush'kal stepped through the doorway. He raised

his hand in greeting and Alexi did the same. A broad smile crossed Mush'kal's face and they moved toward one another and exchanged a brief embrace.

A small crowd gathered on the porch and the people spoke in low tones as the reunited friends approached the doorway. The two boys stepped out again and dashed off down the path to spread the word of Alexi's return.

The woman who had tended him when he couldn't see took him by the arm and led him into the house. Mush'kal relieved him of his bundle and his lance.

The warmth swept over Alexi and brought tears to his eyes. The smells of cooking food and the life in the house filled his senses as he took a seat near the hearth.

He was served stew and he slurped it greedily, smiling as the juices dribbled down his chin. The people gathered around to pat him on the back and welcome him home. A short time later the hit s'aati came from behind his screen. He was wrapped in a fur robe and walked slowly toward Alexi. Alexi rose and looked into the hit s'aati's dark brown eyes. The hit s'aati spoke a short speech to Alexi and Mush'kal translated.

"Welcome home, my young friend," Mush'kal began from behind him. "We had given you over to the spirit world. Now you have come home to us and we are happy. Your presence brings warmth to our house."

The hit s'aati smiled broadly as he listened to Mush'kal translate his speech.

"Gunalcheesh," Alexi replied in Tlingit, "I am pleased to be back."

With that, the hit s'aati walked past Alexi and left the house.

People from the other houses came to visit and Alexi was prompted by Mush'kal to share his story.

Alexi recounted the tale, starting with the journey to the inlet with the boys. He described the hunt and how they had divided into pairs to stalk the deer. Alexi explained how he and his partner had decided to split up. He had strayed too far and found himself in a meadow at the top of the hill. He spotted a small herd of deer, all of them large bucks, and decided to circle behind them hoping to drive them down the hill to the other boys.

He had gotten turned around on the hill. A heavy snow began to fall and he lost his tracks in the meadow. He feared that calling out would frighten the deer so he remained quiet, trying to find his way back to the shore. The weather finally cleared a bit and he spotted a small patch of the sea in the distance below. As he was making his way down the mountain toward the water he slipped under a deadfall and was knocked out.

When he awoke, the forest was dark and he was nearly frozen. He made a fire and huddled next to it through the long night. When morning came he was cold and hungry and delirious from hitting his head but he pushed down the hill to the water, but when he reached the water he didn't recognize anything.

The blow to his head clouded his mind and he was confused. There was no sign of the canoe and the shoreline was unfamiliar. For several days he walked the shoreline, never finding a sign of the canoe or the other boys.

He ate seaweed and clams and spent the long nights huddled under piles of boughs and grasses. As the days passed, his memory returned and he explored the shoreline near his camp. He found a summer camp and the axe and sleeping mat. They had saved his life. He described his trek along the shore, walking to the end of Bear Bay. The weather turned bitter cold and he huddled in his camp, journeying to the water only for his meals.

Everyone was suddenly quiet when he told of how the otter had come to him on the beach. When he said the otter had led him to cross the channel, the audience whispered to one another as Mush'kal translated.

Alexi took the lance and showed how he had killed the deer and enjoyed his first meal of venison. Alexi finished the account of his adventure and smiled at his audience.

One of the men who had been sitting quietly at the back of the group made a speech and everyone turned to listen. When he had finished, he motioned Mush'kal to translate.

"The hit s'aati's nephew says you were visited by a Kushtakah," Mush'kal told him. "The Kushtakah sometimes saves a special person from death in the sea. You are a fortunate to have been looked upon favorably by the spirit of the land otter."

Alexi nodded agreement with the speaker and sat at the hearth answering questions. Soon the crowd dispersed and he was left with Mush'kal enjoying the warmth of the cooking fire.

Chapter 30

Alexi again fell into the winter life of the Tlingit and the days grew longer and warmer. He spent the days paddling along the shores around the village. On many of his voyages, he practiced loading and shooting the long guns, improving his marksmanship. He shot several more seal from his kayak, returning to a noisy welcome from the young boys in the village each time.

The herring that had abandoned the bay through the winter months, suddenly returned one day, and a wave of excitement swept through the village. The herring had moved to their spawning grounds, and the village would follow to collect the spawn. Alexi went with the people of the Shark House, half a day's journey to a small bay bounded by a long wooded spit and a small island. The women and children gathered long ribbons of kelp on the shoreline and the younger men cut hemlock branches from the forest and spread them over the shore at low tide, anchoring them with heavy stones.

The bay teemed with life. The schools of herring swarmed in the water near the shore and the water turned milky white. Every bird imaginable gathered to feast upon the delicate eggs. When the tide receded, the branches and kelp leaves were covered in thick layers of tiny translucent spheres. The rubbery eggs were eaten right off of the branches and kelp. The women cut the egg-covered branches and seaweed into strips and layered it in cedar boxes. Between the layers, they packed fresh hemlock boughs.

The Shark House filled a dozen boxes and heaped the center of two of the large canoes with the remaining bounty. In less than a week's time they returned to the village. The people from the other houses returned in nearly the same way, and traded stories of the harvest from their favorite places.

The village enjoyed a feast with dancing and singing for two nights. Alexi faced the three young men from the deer hunt on the second night. None of them would look him in the eye. He moved away, sparing them the shame of their betrayal.

Following the egg harvest, the weather grew warmer and the people began to spend more time out of doors. Several hunting parties went for spring seals.

One morning when the sun shone brightly on the snow-capped mountains, the hit s'aati came with Mush'kal to Alexi and made a speech.

"The people of the Shark House will travel to the village of the Sit'ka. You will make the journey with us," Mush'kal translated the most beautiful words Alexi had ever heard.

"When will we go?" Alexi asked.

"Preparations have begun. In a few days the house will depart. There will be favorable tides on the half moon," his friend explained.

"Will you go on this trip?" Alexi asked.

"I will travel with the house on this journey," Mush'kal replied.

"I am glad of that," Alexi said.

New Archangel

Chapter 31

The preparations for the journey went quickly and on a cloudy morning at low tide, they set out. Two large canoes carried ten people each, and four smaller canoes carried four. Wolf Boy and another boy from his uncle's house were in one of the large canoes.

Alexi paddled his kayak among the canoes, carrying his belongings in his boat. They followed the eastern shore of Bear Bay and the village soon disappeared from sight. Alexi felt a great sadness as the village vanished behind him.

The tide swept them along the shore and they covered a large stretch of the bay on the first day. Alexi recognized his camps as they passed them and was reminded of his journey. When they reached the narrow passage where he had crossed the bay, he paused as he recalled his encounter with the otter. Had the otter truly come to him to save his life? He could not doubt what the man at the fire had said.

They set up a camp on the shore near the end of the inlet and laughed about sore and tired muscles. A box of herring eggs and seal oil was opened and everyone dined on eggs dipped in oil. The people practiced their stories and dances for the celebration that would be enjoyed when they reached the Sit'ka village.

In the morning the party paddled a short distance and reached the marshy end of Bear Bay. The canoes were beached and their cargo was unloaded onto the shore.

"We will portage the canoes through the forest," Mush'kal explained.

Alexi was confused. "Why would we take the canoes into the woods?" he asked his friend as they carried boxes.

"Tenakee Bay is just through the trees, it will save much paddling and we will travel on protected waters," Mush'kal explained.

Alexi nodded and fell silent as they all worked to unload the canoes for the portage.

When the canoes were empty, the men cut boughs from a spruce tree, trimmed them down to the length of a man's arm and removed their bark. The logs were spaced on the ground in front of the first large canoe and the men put their backs into sliding the canoe onto the logs. Once it started moving, the canoe slid easily over the logs and young boys took turns carrying the log that emerged behind the canoe to the front to continue the skidding. The passage through the woods was short and soon the canoe slid into the water on the opposite shore. A long and narrow inlet stretched to the east, its protected waters calm in the morning sun.

The remaining canoes were portaged in similar fashion and Alexi had the help of two of the men to carry his loaded kayak across the portage. By midday the fleet had reloaded and was paddling down Tenakee bay.

The weather held and the party had a pleasant ride out of Tenakee Bay. They left the long bay and paddled for one day along the shore of a wide strait that stretched away to north and south as far as the eye could see. The waters of the strait were choppy and Alexi was wet much of the time. On the afternoon of the third day they turned inland up a narrow inlet. In the evening they made their camp on the bank of a small river in a tiny bay tucked into the north side of the inlet. The men in one of the small canoes had killed a seal the previous day and they dined on a stew of boiled seal and herring eggs mixed with cockles and seaweed gathered from the shore. Alexi enjoyed the songs and the dance.

In the late morning of the following day, the boats were pulled up on the shore where the channel narrowed to the width of a large river. The tide had begun to run and the water in the channel was turbulent and noisy.

"We will wait here for the tide to ease," Mush'kal explained as they sat on the shore. "The water of the narrows is very dangerous on a strong tide. Many canoes have swamped in this passage."

"I need the rest," Alexi answered.

He had grown weary as the days had passed. He was eating well, but they had covered a great distance. Having many paddlers in the canoes allowed each of them some rest, but he had to paddle his kayak alone.

The people of the Shark House spread out along the shore and sat in small groups visiting and resting as they waited for the water to calm.

The sky was sprinkled with puffs of clouds and the sun found its way through now and then. Wolf Boy crouched near the water not far down the shore. He had kept his distance. Mush'kal told Alexi that people from the village had searched for him when he had not returned. But Mush'kal now knew that the boys had taken the search party to the wrong place, knowing Alexi would not be there.

Alexi sat on the beach near his kayak, watching Wolf Boy. Wolf Boy faced the water, digging in the mud with a stick. Suddenly a mass of brown emerged from the thicket behind him. The bear moved slowly at first and then began to run.

The bear was upon Wolf Boy before Alexi could shout an alarm.

Alexi dashed to his kayak as he yelled to the people on the shore. Everyone looked at him, puzzled by his shouting. Mush'kal rose to his feet in an instant and looked down the shore to where Alexi was pointing as he ran to his kayak. Mush'kal shouted the alarm in Tlingit and the men sprang to their feet.

Alexi had already retrieved his long guns and was running toward Wolf Boy.

The bear tossed Wolf Boy like a doll, moving in circles around the struggling figure. Alexi was soon just a dozen paces from the bear. He set one long gun on the rocks, pulled the other to his shoulder and cocked back the hammer.

The bear heard the click and whirled to face Alexi. Alexi fired directly into the bear's face. The ball ripped flesh from the bear's nose, and took one of its eyes. The bear stood up on its hind legs. Towering over Wolf Boy's limp body the huge animal pawed at its injured face with pads as large as a man's head. The bear let out a low, deep growl. Alexi dropped the first long gun and shouldered the second. A blast ripped from the barrel and the ball shattered the bear's heart. The animal dropped to all fours and lunged toward the alders. The bear fell, heaving in the grass, blood pouring from its mouth.

The men of the Shark House stood over the body of Wolf Boy to protect him from further attack. Several had long guns, others had only spears. Alexi shook like a leaf in a strong wind. He dropped to his knees and set the long gun on the rocks. He vomited and struggled to catch his breath.

Mush'kal knelt beside him. He held Alexi tightly by the shoulders. Alexi turned to look at Wolf Boy. His hair was matted with blood and his deer skin shirt and trousers were torn and soaked with blood. The men hovered over the injured boy and spoke to him in low tones.

Several women began to treat Wolf Boy. The men moved away and let the women take over. The women cut away the shredded clothing and washed Wolf Boy's wounds in seawater. Alexi became sick again and then was helped to his feet by Mush'kal and two of the other men. They gathered his long guns and walked back to the canoes. Several men had already pushed the hit s'aati's canoe off of the beach and were paddling toward the group on the beach.

Alexi sat beside his kayak and watched as Wolf Boy was lifted into the canoe by the hit s'aati and some of the other men. They pushed the canoe into the water and set off down the channel, leaving the beach deserted. The people that remained on the shore spoke in hushed tones and made ready to depart. The bear would lie where it had fallen.

The rest of the people loaded into the remaining canoes and made their way into the narrows. The tide had slackened and the water was calm as they made the passage. The shoreline was lined by low cliffs. Several deer were feeding on new grass growing below the alders. Alexi numbly followed the canoes. The shock and fear of the encounter with the bear had passed and he was exhausted. He wanted to talk with Mush'kal but didn't want to disturb the somber mood.

They left the narrow passage behind and were making their way southwest in a wide channel when the light began to fade. They made camp and ate a quiet meal of dried halibut. Alexi lay in his bedroll, listening to the hushed conversations around the fire.

The next morning was spent working through a narrow channel scattered with small islands and braided passages. The boats moved single file, behind the lead of the smallest canoe. At mid-day the channel opened into a broad sound. The familiar cone of the volcano appeared from behind a wooded point and tears welled in Alexi's eyes. He was home.

Chapter 32

The Sit'ka village was two leagues north of New Archangel. In all of the time Alexi had paddled the sound, he had never ventured toward the village, but now he found himself welcomed by the people that were so feared by the Russians.

As the boats pulled up on the shore they were surrounded by the people of the village who were dressed in ceremonial regalia. The hit s'aati's canoe floated just off of the shore, anchored in the shallow channel. The welcome speeches were skipped due to Wolf Boy's dire circumstance.

Mush'kal met Alexi and explained that Wolf Boy was badly wounded and had not yet awakened, but the shaman was confident that his patient would recover. Mush'kal told Alexi that the hit s'aati knew the true story of how Alexi had been lost in the forest.

"Wolf Boy told his uncle the truth. The shaman says the bear was sent to remind Wolf Boy of the importance of harmony," Mush'kal explained to Alexi. "The hit s'aati says go to your father now, return in two days for the celebration if you wish."

"Thank you," Alexi took his friend's arm and turned toward the shoreline. He looked at the Tlingit people gathered on the beach and felt great sadness at leaving. He pushed his kayak into the water and paddled south. His stomach was in knots as he drew near the fort.

The sun was high overhead as Alexi paddled his kayak into the harbor at New Archangel. Three ships stood at anchor and the docks were busy with the unloading of a fourth. The voices, speaking in his beloved Russian, drifted like music across the calm water. He slipped unnoticed between the stern of the ship and the pier.

The gravel beach on which he had long ago abandoned his small kayak was empty. He nosed into the beach and stepped onto the shore. He was home.

Alexi pulled the kayak up the beach and slipped his paddle beneath the deck. He lashed the lead to the iron ring and climbed to the path.

Alexi forced himself to move slowly, fighting the urge to run wildly up the path to his father's shop. He wanted to do just that but he didn't want to shock his father. He formed another plan. He would go quietly to the church and consult Father Nikolai. The priest would break the news of his return to his father and they would be happily reunited.

The people of the fort were busy and took no notice of Alexi as he walked along the muddy path. The church was situated where the two main paths crossed and was a welcome sight to Alexi. He made his way along the path and stopped at the doorway.

He listened for several minutes, realizing that he had no idea what day it was. Perhaps there was a Sunday service being conducted. School might be in session but it seemed too quiet. Alexi pushed open the heavy wooden doors and stepped into the darkened foyer. He called softly to the priest and heard a faint reply from the far end of the building.

He followed the voice and stopped in the doorway of Father Nikolai's library. He rapped lightly on the door and the father called for him to enter.

"Come, come, it's open," the father said without looking

up from his manuscript.

"Father, I've come home," Alexi said.

Father Nikolai, high priest of the church at New Archangel, looked up at Alexi and his jaw fell open. The priest sat speechless for a long while. He rubbed his eyes and looked again.

"I cannot believe… what my eyes are showing me," the priest said as he rose and walked around his large desk to the ragged figure that stood before him.

"Your face is the same but the boy I last saw in September is gone. He who stands before me now is surely a man," Father Nikolai reached out his hand and touched Alexi on his sleeve.

"What can you tell me of my father?" Alexi regretted the abrupt question. His patience was near its end. He had been gone from New Archangel for more than half of a year, and he longed for his father's company.

"Will you tell him of my arrival?" Alexi asked. "I don't want to shock him with news I am still counted among the living."

"Sit my son," Father Nikolai motioned him to a heavy chair beside his desk. "Sit down and let me tell you of things in New Archangel."

"Please, Father," Alexi protested, "will you bring the news of my arrival to my father or must I see to it myself?"

"My son, I am sorry to tell you that your father is gone," the priest sat on the front of the desk. He extended his arm and placed a hand firmly on Alexi's shoulder.

Alexi shrank into the chair, the priest's words knocked the wind from him.

"Gone? Do you mean dead?" he blurted out, tears welling in his eyes.

"No. No my son. He left New Archangel and returned to

Russia," the priest was quick to reassure him. "He traveled on the last ship of the season. They departed at the end of October. When the news of your loss came, he no longer had an interest in service to the company and terminated his contract. He sailed on the *Neva* with the last load of fur."

Alexi dropped his head into his hands and was silent, his disappointment overwhelmed him. After a moment he raised his head, ready to continue talking to the priest.

"What became of the crew of the *Irena*?" Alexi inquired.

"A sad, sad tale," the Father continued. "One of the boats was swamped soon after they abandoned the crippled ship, and all hands were drowned. The boats had become separated in the terrible sea and there was no chance for rescue by the other boat. The second boat managed to make a safe passage behind a barrier island where they waited out the storm. When the weather broke they sailed south and made New Archangel in a weeks' time. Four of the men were badly injured and the surgeon was only able to save two of them. The captain and mate were on the launch that foundered and the position of the *Irena* was lost."

"None among those who returned could account for you," the priest explained. "They spoke of the broken main mast crushing the galley. You and the cook were thought to have died in the wreck."

"I buried the cook on an island," Alexi spoke of his departed friend for the first time since he had left the island.

Alexi recounted his story for the priest and suggested that he could recover the cargo of furs for the company if Governor Baranov would arrange passage to Russia to join his father.

"I am afraid that the Governor sailed shortly after your father," Father Nikolai informed him of a second unexpected change. "His health was failing and he grew weary of the constant battles with the Company owners in St. Petersburg. I am sorry to say that word returned on the first ship this season that the Governor died on the voyage."

Alexi was stunned. Governor Baranov *was* New Archangel, he ruled with an iron fist tempered by a kind heart. He had shown Alexi and his father great kindness through the years. It was Governor Baranov who had arranged his scholarship to the Naval Academy.

"Governor Khlebnikov now oversees the operations of the company," the priest said. "I am sure he will be happy to hear your story and offer you a settlement for your difficulties and the return of company property."

The priest returned to his seat behind the desk and sat silently while he allowed Alexi to digest the news.

"Let us go to the new Governor now," Alexi suggested.

"I think that is a good idea," the priest agreed. "Perhaps I can convince you that a bath and some new clothes might be of use?"

Alexi looked himself over in the long mirror that hung in a dark wooden frame on the wall across the room. He could scarcely believe his eyes. Staring back at him was the lanky figure of a young man. His clothes were tattered and uniformly blackened. The Tlingit had provided him deerskin trousers and jersey to replace the tattered rags he had worn when he fled the ship. He retained his canvas coat and it had held up well. Alexi walked closer to the mirror and studied his face carefully. A thin mustache had begun to darken the skin beneath his nose. His dark and dirty face was framed by a tangle of shoulder length hair and though he couldn't detect his aroma, the look the priest had on his face told him it had not gone unnoticed.

"A bath and some new clothes would suit me fine," Alexi agreed to the Father's suggestion.

It was early evening before the priest and his freshly-washed guest walked the darkened path from the church to the Governor's house high on the hill overlooking the fort. The men who were gathered for drinks before the evening meal listened in fascination as Alexi recounted his tale.

One of the men was the captain of a Yankee merchant ship bound for Kodiak in three days' time. He offered to take Alexi aboard as his guest and serve as steward for the lost cargo of furs, should they recover them. He invited Alexi to visit him on his ship, the *Reliant*, as soon as Alexi was settled.

Alexi enjoyed a splendid meal of roast pork and pickled eggs. He took his leave with Father Nikolai and spent the night in the church. Alexi slept fitfully under warm quilts. Dreams of his father and the bear attacking Wolf Boy filled his sleep. He awoke before any in the church had begun to stir and sat and stared out a small window at a starry sky.

The sadness and disappointment of having to wait to be reunited with his father, and word of the death of Baranov were heavy on his heart. When Alexi heard Father Nikolai moving in his chambers, he joined the priest for tea and bread and then took his leave.

Chapter 33

In the early morning light, with a damp chill in the air, Alexi slipped out of the fort and launched his kayak. He made for the narrows north of the fort and before the sun crested the hill, he was within sight of the Sit'ka village. Smoke rose from the roofs of the long houses but there were no signs of life. He paddled past the line of canoes.

Alexi drifted with the tide. A pair of loons whistled, their eerie call echoing through the trees. When Alexi returned to the sleepy village, the people had begun to stir. A group of young men who were conversing on the shore moved toward him as he pulled his kayak onto the beach.

The men greeted him in Tlingit, and he returned the greeting. They motioned him to follow and they entered the Sit'ka Shark House. Alexi was welcomed and they inquired about his father. When they heard his story they were saddened. Alexi learned that Wolf Boy had awakened and his wounds showed little sign of festering. The shaman's medicine was strong. As they sat by the fire sharing stories, the hit s'aati of the Sit'ka Shark House approached Alexi.

He spoke through Mush'kal.

"Tonight we will enjoy a feast and I invite you to join our celebration," the hit s'aati made his invitation.

"I will be honored to join you," Alexi replied.

Alexi spent the day with the people of the village, enjoying the contests and the singing. Many of the young men stopped to admire his kayak and asked questions about his journey.

When evening came, the people of Huna joined their hosts in their long house for an evening of feasting and gifting. The hit s'aati of both houses made long speeches and told their favorite stories. The men and women shared stories and the clans sang songs back and forth.

The food was delicious. Meats and eggs, seaweed delicacies and dried salmon and halibut were served in plentiful quantities. Finally Mush'kal called Alexi to the hearth in the middle of the room and sat him on a large cedar box draped with a beaver pelt. The hit s'aati came and stood beside Alexi and made a speech to everyone in the house as they sat huddled close, listening intently.

"Late in the Season of the Goose my son and his cousins, made their first journey to the Bay of Ice to hunt seal. A great wave came upon them and they spilled from their canoe."

The hit s'aati paused for a moment and the people in the audience whispered amongst themselves. "Only my son survived, and clung to life in the water. This boy," he motioned toward Alexi, "happened upon Wolf Boy and took him to the shore and warmed him by his fire."

The storyteller pointed to the fire pit and waved his hands over the flickering flames. "I and some of the men from our village searched for them when they failed to return. In the fading light we spotted a fire on the shore near a summer fish camp."

He continued, "We stole up to the camp and discovered this boy sleeping by his fire. He was trespassing and I prepared to dispatch him with my club," he reached behind a second box and retrieved his war club.

The crowd murmured as the hit s'aati raised the club above his head, the muscles in his powerful arms rippling.

"As I swung my club, I heard my son's voice and I tried to stop but could not. Wolf Boy lay wrapped under furs in this boy's shelter," the hit s'aati paused. "This son of the Russians was brought to our village to be the guest of the Shark House. He received nursing from my daughters and the shaman. He has been the guest of our house this long winter and has joined us on our journey, returning to his village to find his father," the hit s'aati stopped and looked at Alexi.

"On our journey to this village, my son was attacked by a bear. It was by the bravery of this young man that he was again saved from death," the hit s'aati waited as Alexi's deed was discussed among the crowd. Many pointed to Alexi.

"The people of the Shark House are grateful to Alexi for his kindness, I wish to give you a gift that will last as a memory of your family in the village of Huna," the hit s'aati said. "Your friend Mush'kal, our friend and servant would be lost without you and you without him."

The translation flowed from Mush'kal's mouth just as it had since Alexi first arrived at the Huna village. It took a moment for the words he had heard and then spoken to make sense. When they did, Mush'kal turned to face Alexi, tears welling in his eyes.

The hit s'aati laughed and clapped Mush'kal on the back. "You are free."

Alexi understood the answer in Tlingit and felt his breath leave him in a heavy sigh. He hugged the friend who had been his voice among the Tlingit and they sat together on the cedar box. The celebration resumed and there was generous gifting. Every guest down to the smallest child received a gift of some kind. The women favored strips of colored cloth and the men enjoyed gifts of carved implements and hunting gear.

Alexi received a number of beaver and mink pelts as well

as a knife and a bundle of dried salmon for his journey. The dancing, singing and storytelling continued into the wee hours of the morning and when the celebration was finally over, everyone slept soundly in the warmth of the long house.

Chapter 34

In the morning Alexi bid farewell to his Tlingit friends. At the request of Wolf Boy, Alexi and Mush'kal visited the injured Tlingit. Wolf Boy lay on a bed of hides and was covered with a sea otter blanket. His voice was weak when he spoke. "Forgive me, Alexi. I did not deserve your kindness."

"Everyone deserves kindness," Alexi replied, "I wish you a long life, Wolf Boy," They both smiled and Alexi grasped the outstretched hand of the young man who had once wished him dead. Wolf Boy closed his eyes and rested.

Two of the Huna men paddled Mush'kal and the gifts Alexi had received as far as the first dock at the edge of the fort and departed quickly. Alexi paddled the kayak onto the shore and joined Mush'kal. It took several trips to carry their belongings to the head of the dock.

The *Reliant* tugged at her moorings, her crew moving about the deck as the cargo and supplies for the voyage to Kodiak were stowed. Alexi caught the eye of the captain who strode across the deck and joined Alexi and Mush'kal on the pier.

"Good day, gentlemen," the captain greeted them. "Bring your gear aboard and make yourselves at home. There are empty bunks in the foc'sle. I hope you can sleep in a cramped space."

"Thank you, yes," Alexi replied. "We'll move our things

there now if it is convenient."

"Yes, yes. We sail on the morning tide. Best you get settled and get some sleep," the captain suggested, "of course you will be called upon to help with the sailing."

"With pleasure, sir," Alexi agreed.

"You can stow your baidarka along the aft rail," the captain pointed to the stern of the ship where a heavy rail capped thick bulwarks.

Alexi smiled as he recalled finding his kayak in the same place on the *Irena* so long ago.

Mush'kal was quiet and stood behind Alexi as he spoke to the captain. He listened and took in the sights and sounds of the harbor. It had been many seasons since Mush'kal had seen the fort.

They carried their belongings aboard the ship and stowed the kayak. The crew stopped and stared as they loaded the skin boat. They had all heard the story of the shipwrecked boy and his winter with the Tlingit. There was admiration and curiosity in their stares.

When all of the gear was stored, Alexi left Mush'kal on the ship and made his way along the sloppy streets to the church.

Father Nikolai waited for him, and several of his friends from the school were gathered to wish him well. He shook their hands and retold his story. They listened intently, asking questions as he spun the tale. When Alexi finished recounting his adventure, Father Nikolai sent the children on their way and invited Alexi into the library. On the table lay a map and a letter, sealed with the stamp of the Russian American Company in red wax.

"In this envelope is a letter detailing your payment for the recovery of the *Irena's* fur if you are successful. The map is for you to modify as you see fit based on your observations both past and future," the priest explained the documents. "Give this document to the company representative in Kodiak and he will draft a note for the bank in St. Petersburg. It has been arranged for you to attend the Naval Academy in St. Petersburg, on scholarship, as was Baranov's intention. He would have been most proud to have known of your adventures."

Alexi took the documents and looked at the priest.

"Do you think I will find my father?" Alexi asked his teacher and friend.

"I know you will, and I will pray every day for your success and safety my son," the priest reassured him.

"Thank you Father," Alexi was greatly saddened at his leaving. "Perhaps we will meet again someday."

"Perhaps, and if we do, I'm sure you will have made yourself an example of success for the rest of us to follow," the priest stretched his arms and hugged Alexi close to him. "God bless you my son."

Alexi took his leave and wandered back to the docks. He and Mush'kal worked into the darkness stowing cargo as crewmen on their new ship.

Kamchatka

Chapter 35

The *Reliant* slipped her moorings at first light and was towed clear of the docks. The crew soon had her sails unfurled and she began her voyage on a light easterly breeze. The captain barked orders which the crew happily obeyed. Soon the merchant ship was cutting through choppy seas on a heading to clear the cape beneath the volcano.

Heavy gray clouds crowded the horizon. As they left the sound behind, Alexi prayed for a safe journey. He recalled his first voyage all too well and wished for no such adventure any time soon.

The captain steered a course for the latitude he had worked out based on the reports from the crew of the *Irena*, and the descriptions Alexi provided. With a favorable southeast wind and gentle seas, they made the shoreline near the wreck in four days.

On the morning of the fifth day, the sun burned its way through the gray blanket and the snow covered mountains appeared. Alexi felt instantly at home. The tall peak and the blaze on the mountain were visible through the captain's spyglass, and Alexi directed the ship closer to the shore.

The sea was unusually calm and the *Reliant* was able to furl her sails and drift easily a league off of the rocks. The crew launched a longboat and Alexi's kayak was lowered into the water. Mush'kal accompanied six of the crew in the longboat and Alexi led the way toward the breaking surf.

Alexi recalled perfectly the entrance to his tiny harbor and the men in the boat followed him with confidence, his story having been told many times during the voyage. The island was just as he had left it, and they landed on the shore by his camp.

Alexi led the men into the forest. His shelter had collapsed under the heavy snow. He scouted into the forest behind the camp and found the bundles of fur hanging like sausage links from the high branches.

Mush'kal and other crewmen joined him and he climbed the tree and cut down the bundles of fur. The crewmen made three trips to carry the furs, and it was decided that a second trip would be needed to bring all of the fur to the ship. Alexi gave Mush'kal use of his kayak, and Mush'kal fairly leapt into the small boat as he moved to lead the longboat back to the ship.

Alexi remained on the shore, alone on his island. He picked up the single piece of cargo the longboat had brought ashore and stood it on its sharpened point. The iron cross was heavy and bore an inscription, hastily carved by the chisel of the new blacksmith.

Peter Ilyich Vincent

A friend and father

He carried the cross to his friend's grave. The rocks were still neatly piled, but the wooden marker he had fashioned was gone. He loosened some of the stones at the end of the pile and drove the iron cross into the beach. The cross stood upright and he piled large stones around its base until he was certain nothing could move it. Alexi stepped back and crossed himself.

"Goodbye my friend," Alexi said aloud. "Sleep well."

He walked back to his camp. Mush'kal and the crew in the longboat soon returned and they loaded the remaining fur and departed the island. As they paddled away, Alexi gave a long last look at his island and then slipped between the rock cliffs and made for the *Reliant*.

The *Reliant* sailed westward on light winds for six days before the white peaks of the mountains behind Kodiak came into view. The captain told Alexi that Kodiak was one day's sail away.

The island he had sighted early in the morning grew larger with each passing moment. Rounded hills, topped with a thick blanket of snow rose sharply from the sea, ringed with jagged cliffs. Seabirds of all shapes and sizes flew around the ship, floating gracefully in the currents behind the billowing sails. The fort at Kodiak was sighted in late afternoon and Alexi and Mush'kal were anxious to explore.

Three ships were at anchor in the harbor and the docks were busy with two more transferring cargo. The *Reliant* dropped her anchor beyond the other ships and launched a boat. The captain, his mate and three of the crew went ashore to negotiate space at the pier. Alexi spent the evening lying in his bunk, thinking of the next leg of his journey, anxious to secure passage to Kamchatka. He barely slept.

The next morning the *Reliant* weighed anchor and the longboats towed her into a mooring at the largest of the piers. It was the Russian American Company dock and an agent of the company greeted them as they came alongside the pier. He inspected the cargo as it was removed from the holds and made marks on his list as he hurried about the pier and deck of the ship. As the furs were unloaded, they were carried into the company warehouse. The men in the warehouse undid the bundles of fur Alexi had so carefully wrapped the previous fall and spread them over large wooden tables for inspection.

"Magnificent!" the agent exclaimed after a long and tedious inspection. "These furs will bring a fortune in the market at Canton. Young man, come with me and we will see to your payment," he invited Alexi to his offices.

Alexi and the agent discussed the voyage from New Archangel and the fate of Governor Baranov. When Alexi pressed for knowledge of his father, the agent assured him that he was certain the man Alexi described had taken a passage to Petropavlovsk the previous fall.

Alexi made a single request in addition to his payment and the agent was happy to oblige. When the two had concluded their business, the agent presented Alexi with a note of settlement for his care of the furs and a pouch of coins for his travels. Alexi studied the numbers on the note but could not understand its value. He had little knowledge of money. His father had provided all he had ever needed and he had just managed a winter on nothing more than his own resources. He accepted the note and thanked the agent for the coins then took his leave.

When Alexi returned to the pier, Mush'kal stood with all of their belongings stacked neatly beside the kayak.

Alexi smiled and waved to his friend, showing him the note and coins and explaining what he had learned from the agent. The captain of the *Reliant* noticed him from the deck of the ship and joined them on the pier.

"I hope they have rewarded you handsomely?" the captain queried him

"Beyond my expectations," Alexi spoke the truth.

"I have arranged for you to travel to Petropavlovsk aboard the *Fedorova II*. She will sail in one week. The captain and I are good friends from our pirate days," he winked at Alexi.

"Thank you sir, for your kindness and assistance," Alexi replied to the captain who had shown him so much favor.

"It was my pleasure young man." The captain winked and smiled as he reached out his hand. "It isn't every day that a hero of Russia serves as crewman on my ship."

The Captain shook hands with Alexi and Mush'kal and then left them standing on the dock.

Alexi and Mush'kal spent their remaining time in Kodiak exploring the shores and forest surrounding the busy port. They slept in a small room behind the company warehouse and kept to themselves.

Chapter 36

The *Fedorova II* had been at sea for twelve days, sailing west by southwest on a strong wind. Twice the wind had risen to a gale and the crew had been forced to trim the sails and run before massive waves. The *Fedorova II* was the pride of the Russian fleet, with twenty safe crossings to her credit. The Company trusted the captain and crew with its most valuable cargo. A load of fur filled her generous holds. The long swells lifted the massive ship steadily up and down.

At mid-day a large island came into view and the crew trimmed the sails. Lush green grasses carpeted the steep hillsides and stretched to the tops of black cliffs that plunged into the sea. Only the highest tops of the mountains were covered by snow. The ship slowed and made a course change, heading for the island.

From the moment the island appeared, Mush'kal had been standing at the bow rail. Something stirred in him that pushed everything else from his mind. He stared into the distance at the approaching island with the intensity of a mother bear watching over newborn cubs. As the island loomed, a cluster of huts came into view.

A small bay opened into the ragged shoreline, large enough to harbor a single ship. The captain guided the ship through the narrow entrance to the bay, following a longboat, which took soundings to measure the water's depth.

Men and women lined the shore and stared across the water at the approaching ship. Four two-hole kayaks were launched and made their way toward the ship. Two of the kayaks carried a single paddler; the other two held two men.

Alexi approached his friend and touched him on the sleeve. Mush'kal jumped and turned to face Alexi, tears flowing down his cheeks.

"Do you know this place?" Alexi smiled at his friend.

"Yes," Mush'kal replied.

"We have come to bring you home my friend," Alexi replied and hugged Mush'kal around his shoulders.

"Thank you, thank you," Mush'kal hugged Alexi tightly.

The kayaks came alongside the ship and a man shouted in the Unanga tongue to the men at the rail. Two of the Unanga crewmen shouted back to the boats. A rope ladder was lowered over the rail. Two of the paddlers left their kayaks and climbed to the deck.

When the first of the Unanga men stood firmly on the deck, he greeted the captain and then looked about the deck. His eyes passed quickly over the crew then snapped back to Mush'kal. The man rushed across the deck and stood face to face with Mush'kal and looked him over carefully.

The Unanga spoke a few words to which Mush'kal replied. The visitor whooped loudly, the sudden outburst startled everyone on deck. The visitor from the shore embraced Mush'kal so tightly that Alexi thought he might break Mush'kal's ribs. The two men stood holding one another for a long time.

Finally the Unanga turned to the other man who had boarded with him and spoke several long bursts. The man at the rail shouted down to the men in the boats and they shouted back in reply.

When the men had finished with their exchanges,

Mush'kal spoke to Alexi.

"This man is the son of my sister," he told Alexi. "He was only a child when I was taken from my home."

He held the palm of his hand near the deck to show the size of his nephew when he had last seen him.

Mush'kal and Alexi went below and Mush'kal collected his belongings. Alexi motioned Mush'kal to wait for a moment and retrieved one of his long guns from a locker at the forepeak.

"Take this and remember me when you hunt seal," he held the long gun out to Mush'kal with both hands. Mush'kal took the long gun and stepped to him and hugged him like a bear.

"I owe you my life," he said softly to Alexi.

"You owe me nothing. You have given me your friendship," Alexi replied.

"I will always be your friend Mush'kal, now go and enjoy your people once more," Alexi waved him in the direction of the ladder.

"But what of you?" Mush'kal asked.

"I will find my family soon, and then I too will be happy," Alexi replied.

Alexi and Mush'kal emerged from the foc'sle and crossed to the rail. Mush'kal gave his belongings to the Unanga men. The three men waved to Alexi and the crew as they climbed over the rail and descended to their kayaks.

The people on the shore were waving to the ship as it made for open water. Alexi stood at the stern rail and waved to the people on the shore.

The ship made the final passage to Kamchatka with fair winds. The captain remarked that it had been the most pleasant voyage he had ever made between Alaska and Kamchatka. The ship slipped past islands ringed with rugged cliffs and topped by the cones of volcanoes. Several of them spewed wisps of steam from their jagged peaks.

The coastline of Kamchatka looked much like the shores of Alaska. The crew made preparations for a landing at Petropavlovsk, the greatest port in Kamchatka and the gateway to Russia. As they approached the southern tip of the peninsula, snow-covered mountains towered behind low rolling hills that flanked black beaches. The port of Petropavlovsk was nestled against the base of one of these low hills and was flanked on both sides by snow-capped peaks.

They sailed into the busy harbor on a beautiful sunny day. The wind was light and Alexi could feel the warmth of the sun on his face, a sure sign that spring had arrived. The buildings that lined the roads were painted uniformly white and the onion dome of the Orthodox Church rose above the houses and offices beyond the waterfront. It seemed a much grander city than Kodiak and New Archangel.

The *Fedorova* II waited two days for her turn at the docks and was made fast under a gray sky and steady drizzle. Alexi labored with the crew unloading the cargo, happy to work as payment for his passage. When the ship had been relieved of her goods, Alexi offloaded his belongings and stored them in the kayak.

The captain had instructed Alexi to seek out the company agent in the offices at the head of the docks and make him aware of his arrival. The agent would provide him with assistance in making his way.

Alexi stood on the dock and watched the people of Petropavlovsk as they swarmed over the pier, scurrying about their business.

Two small boys happened along and Alexi offered them a silver coin if they would watch over his kayak and belongings while he tended to his business. They eagerly accepted the offer and he left them guarding the small boat like it was their prize pig.

Amazed by the number of people on the docks, Alexi weaved his way toward a tiny building that flew the flag of the Russian American Company. He approached the offices and looked about for signs of an agent. Seeing no one, he opened the door and stepped into a darkened office. A kettle of water steamed silently on a cast iron stove. A tiny silver bell sat on the counter and Alexi shook the bell lightly and waited.

Presently, a round man dressed in a leather apron and a white blouse emerged from a room behind the counter.

"Yes, yes, what is it? I'm a very busy man," he blustered, scarcely giving Alexi a glance.

Alexi greeted him and spread the note from the agent in Kodiak on the counter beneath the man's large red nose. The agent paused and suddenly took a great deal of interest in the note.

"Well, what have we here?" he was noticeably more cordial.

The agent unfolded the paper, holding it close to his face. He muttered to himself as he read, disbelieving its contents.

"My young man, I must apologize. I was unaware of your standing with the company. Please accept my welcome to the fair city of Petropavlovsk," the agent said. "I will send a dispatch to St. Petersburg. Your funds will await you there. In the meantime, how may I be of service to you?"

"I need to find my way to Magadan. I have business there with the family of a departed friend," Alexi spoke of the cook's wife and sons.

"I can put you in contact with the master of a ship that can carry you there," the agent answered. "Will you be seeking lodging in Petropavlovsk for your stay?"

"I will see to my own accommodation, thank you," Alexi declined the offer. "However, I am most interested in locating my father."

"And how may I assist you in that effort?" the agent asked.

"He sailed here from Kodiak on the last ship last season," Alexi replied.

"You will have to make that inquiry at the customs house on the docks," the agent informed him. "They keep the records of passengers that come and go. I am sure you will learn more there. Please return whenever you like and I will make the arrangements for your passage," the agent offered.

Alexi took the note and thanked the agent. Standing on the boardwalk in front of the office, he studied the boats and ships that rode at anchor and plied the protected harbor.

How magnificent the ports of Europe must be if this lonely port on Kamchatka seems so grand, he thought to himself as he made his way back to the ship.

As Alexi rounded the corner at the end of the warehouse, he drew to a stop. His eyes locked onto a man in a heavy woolen coat, bent at the waist, who was speaking to the boys who guarded his kayak. The man's back was broad and the tilt of his black hat was familiar. Alexi's stomach tensed. He crept forward, approaching the man from behind. As he drew closer, he moved from side to side to gain a better measure of the man.

When Alexi stood two paces behind the man he noted the gray that peppered his thick black hair. The man's shoulders sagged, and he leaned heavily on his right leg. The man in the black coat continued to speak to the two small boys as he examined the skin boat. The guardians of his kayak wore serious expressions. The smaller boy's attention drifted from the man, and his eyes fell on Alexi.

The return of the kayak's owner brought relief to the boy's face, and suddenly the man stopped speaking. He straightened to his full height and the sag in his shoulders vanished. The man followed the child's gaze and he slowly turned to face Alexi.

The color drained from an already pale face that was covered by a thick black beard streaked with gray. Brown eyes came instantly alive as the man in the heavy woolen coat stared at Alexi. Alexi rushed forward and threw his arms around the man's chest. The man squeezed the air from Alexi's lungs.

"Alexi, my son you are alive!" the man sobbed with joy.

"Yes. Yes I am," Alexi told his father.

...The old man looked down on the children. Their eyes were slits that wavered on the edge of slumber. The blond boy smiled when his grandfather's large hands pulled the quilts up under his chin.

"Thank you for that wonderful story Grandpa Alexi," he mumbled.

"Sleep well my little sausages," the old man whispered as he blew out the lamp. **"Sleep well."**

The End

Made in the USA
Columbia, SC
13 May 2018